# PRAISE FOR *WILD, FEARLESS CHESTS*

'A haunting, uncompromising collection, *Wild, Fearless Chests* – stylistically polished, often visceral in effect – offers a bold new voice in the Australian literary culture.' *Australian Book Review*

'Powerfully rhythmic, disjointed, poetic and passionate, referencing such literary beacons as Hemingway, Frame, Kafka, Bukowski with a determined belief in the power of words, a possible escape from despair.' *Sydney Morning Herald*

'*Wild, Fearless Chests* is a visceral tour de force . . . a devastatingly smart collection.' *AU Review*

'You can feel the universe expanding and exhaling with Beaumont's beautifully calibrated prose . . . *Wild, Fearless Chests* is a treasure chest of twenty-one unrelenting and unforgettable stories, shocking and shimmering on first read, rewarding in the re-reading.' *Sydney Arts Guide*

'The tales pack a solid punch, both literal and metaphorical, and Beaumont's voice . . . is resolute. By writing about (young) women in an unashamedly feminist manner, by offering them a way to express their anger, confusion and pain, *Wild, Fearless Chests* is as validating as it is devastating.' *Big Issue*

'"Drowning in Thick Air" is shocking . . . It is not like anything I have read in recent years and takes me a place I have never been in my life or imagination or in fiction.' Frank Moorhouse on 'Drowning in Thick Air' from *Wild, Fearless Chests*

ALSO BY MANDY BEAUMONT

*Wild, Fearless Chests*

# THE FURIES

## MANDY BEAUMONT

hachette
AUSTRALIA

Published in Australia and New Zealand in 2022
by Hachette Australia
(an imprint of Hachette Australia Pty Limited)
Gadigal Country, Level 17, 207 Kent Street, Sydney NSW 2000
www.hachette.com.au

Hachette Australia acknowledges and pays our respects to the past, present and
future Traditional Owners and Custodians of Country throughout Australia
and recognises the continuation of cultural, spiritual and educational practices
of Aboriginal and Torres Strait Islander peoples. Our head office is located on
the lands of the Gadigal people of the Eora Nation.

10 9 8 7 6 5 4 3 2 1

 A catalogue record for this
book is available from the
National Library of Australia

ISBN: 978 0 7336 4307 1 (paperback)

*Lines on page vii from* Ariel *by Sylvia Plath reproduced with permission from Faber and Faber Ltd.*

Cover design by Christabella Designs
Cover photographs courtesy of Trevillion and Shutterstock
Typeset in 12.2/18.7 pt Adobe Garamond Pro by Bookhouse, Sydney
Printed and bound in Australia by McPherson's Printing Group

 The paper this book is printed on is certified against the
Forest Stewardship Council® Standards. McPherson's Printing
Group holds FSC® chain of custody certification SA-COC-005379.
FSC® promotes environmentally responsible, socially beneficial
and economically viable management of the world's forests.

*For Ben, for your Angus. For Russ, for our Shanks.*
*For the losses that shape our futures.*

Out of the ash
I rise with my red hair
And I eat men like air.

—Sylvia Plath, 'Lady Lazarus'


When you come out of the storm, you won't be the same
person who walked in. That's what this storm's all about.

—Haruki Murakami, *Kafka on the Shore*

IN CLASSICAL MYTHOLOGY, the Furies were vengeful female divinities – the daughters of the ancestral mother of all life, Gaia – who ascended from the underworld to pursue and punish the wicked on Earth.

# PREFACE

**A GIRL'S\* GUIDE TO MISPLACEMENT AND NATURAL DISASTERS:**
There is a list. You have one too, don't you? (Yes, you.) Your best
friend does. I do. The woman you have never met does. Mine
is kept in my head, but while drunk one night I wrote all their
names on a piece of foolscap paper; stopped when I got too drunk
to care anymore. I never finished that list, am still not sure if I
can remember all their names or descriptors. These encounters as
I/you/we/your mother/grandmother/your best friend/the woman
you met one night at a party remember them, are not the same
as the way they remember them. These lists are yours/ours/hers.

---

\* Stop calling us girls — we are women.

Are real, and. I. Want. You. To. Know. I really want you to know that we are beginning to use their real names now,* we are all warning our daughters about them, showing our young friends pictures of them, telling them that nowhere is safe to walk anymore. We hold our young sisters to our chests as they cry, and. The ground swells beneath our feet. Do you feel it? Do you see? The. Rivers bursting, the. Pandemics rising, the. Crops and wildlife dying, the. Deep holes swallowing cities on the news? Do you hear the roar, the splutter, the whoosh of fire building to inferno around you? Hear that? Yes. That. Listen. There is no rhythm, no pattern – how very boring if there were. There is, however, a lesson for you about how catastrophe, how sudden and widespread disaster, can be stopped and dismantled. I. Want. You. To. Know. I really want you to know that, if you don't try, the natural world around you – she will destroy you.

---

* Anthony, Bob, Adam.

ONE

# MADE OF GRISTLE

AFTER IT HAPPENED, I'd walk in slow circles outside the house looking for her, my feet hardening and my skin turning a deep brown. My hands a trapped and heated burn. My knees wrapped and seeping. Three months after it happened, my father left me alone with the memory of it all. Left. A house we once called home. Left. A stack of bills, a dinner that I made for him sitting on the dining room table. I was just about to turn sixteen.

When my hands healed and the heat had cooled into a numbing ache, I got a job at the abattoir nearly an hour away from home: the one where my father used to work in the summer, when the cattle couldn't be fed anymore, when men's hopes were dashed.

A last-ditch attempt for money. Feed the kids. Some water in the tank. Fix the back fence. Trucks lined up for kilometres, waiting. Bones sticking out from the beasts' stomachs, their eyes pleading, their moaning grouped as they were herded out into the pens behind the abattoir. Their previous owners driving away with their stomachs grumbling, thinking of sausages and mash for dinner, maybe a bottle of beer snuck in on the drive home.

ON MY FIRST DAY OF WORK, Pat, who knew my father, handed me a sledgehammer and told me that if the cattle didn't die straight-away after you hit them, that they could thrash, could knock a man unconscious. He'd seen it happen before. Legs slipping in their own blood. Men moving around them, their arms raised, the look of fear in their eyes. And Pat laughed, stood close, too close, as the first one fell and I raised the sledgehammer, slammed down hard on its head, its ribs collapsing into a heavy-moaned breath, the air relaxing around its mouth in its final moment, and. Bleach, warm blood, the mighty dead all around us. Pat didn't ask about my father, my mother. Didn't ask about what had happened. On that first day, he stood close enough so I could watch the way his knife moved, the way he held a beast's leg, the way to talk to the other men. And as the knock-off bell went that afternoon, he nodded at me as I walked into the tearoom to punch my card, walked to the long basins to scrub my arms and hose down my boots and my heavy plastic apron. Hang it up. Head down. Don't-look-any-of-them-in-the-eye. Walk outside and light a smoke. Jump in my father's ute and drive home. Feel the dry heat hit my face. Think of all the ways to leave this place, to forget that look on my mother's face the night it happened. That fire. That booming gold. Me running down to her. Run – *I'm coming.* On my hands and knees. The hair on my skin singeing. My father kneeling over, vomit falling from his mouth and already a shadowed sorrow against the dark land behind him. Three men grabbing me. Up. Out. Away. *There's nothing else to do, sweetheart. There's nothing else we can do.*

LATER THAT WEEK, IN THE TEAROOM, a group of young men sit around me, ask if I'm enjoying the job, if the drive in is all right, if the big dam out my way has dried up yet. They don't ask about my mother. They've all seen the news. They've all heard the whispers.

Simon, the youngest of them, stays behind when the others go out for a smoke. He moves next to me and asks if I'll be staying closer to town now that I'm working here. I don't respond. I know what he really wants to ask is how I can stay in a house that holds so much sadness. He tells me that lots of the men live at the local caravan park at this busy time of year. (I imagine their mothers sending them clean clothes, homemade biscuits in the mail, aftershave for those occasions when they drive into the city for the night.) He touches my arm as I get up to go back to work and tells me he'd be happy to come with me to the caravan park to meet the owner, if I want. He says he can meet me at my house just before breakfast tomorrow, that he knows where I live, that he'll get a lift out there from his sister Michelle. *She can swing past on her way to work. She won't mind.*

**THE NEXT MORNING HE'S WALKING DOWN THE DIRT DRIVEWAY** towards the house as I drink the last of my coffee. I've already packed, already moved two boxes to the bottom of the front stairs. Clothes. Toiletries. A gold-framed photo of my sister and me. Her small toy rabbit that she'd called Bunchy after the way his little soft cotton face bunched up together when she held him tight. It's all I'll need from this place, I think. I rinse my cup in the sink as he stands at the bottom of the stairs. And, I'm out the door and down the steps before he can come up. I lean down and grab a box and start walking to my father's white HQ Holden ute. *You're keen for a Saturday morning, Cyn,* he says, half laughing, but more focused on where he is and searching the ground for where it happened, for the charcoaled ash, for police tape, for my father's dried vomit. By the time he lifts his head to ask me about it, I've already put the boxes in the back of the ute and jumped in the driver's seat. He walks to the HQ and jumps in too, starts rolling us both a smoke and puts his feet up on my dashboard like we are going on a date or down the store for a carton of milk. He asks if he can turn on the stereo. I start the engine. *Sure.* He stares at the house, at the garden my mother once planted (dead now), at the land around us that I've always known (flat red land, the mountain behind us, old sheds, trees and small yellowed shrubs reaching for salvation), at the dark spot in the front of the house. The radio blares, and. He coughs once and looks over at me as I put my hand on the gear shift. *Three on the tree, love, three on the tree*, I remember my father telling me when he first taught me to drive, his hands on mine trying to move the gears in a seamless H. Left, up, put it in reverse. All the way down, and I'm in first and driving out the dirt driveway. *Don't look. Don't look back at that spot*, I think to myself. *Smoke your smoke. Eyes on the road. You never have to come back here again.*

AN HOUR LATER, we're pulling into the caravan park, we're pulling our skin off the hot vinyl seats and walking together into the small office behind the main gates. The woman behind the counter is scratching her arse and looking me up and down. The ends of her hair are bleach-blonde-dry and her breasts are large (large, as large as a bag of flour falling-fat over the kitchen bench).

She stands up and nods at Simon, asks me how long I want to stay for, tells me none of the men here are allowed in my caravan after nine. (*A slut just like her mother, probably.*) No weed. No bright lights. No towels or toiletries left in the shared shower block. I'll usually have the ladies all to myself. Not many women stay here. (*Slut.*) I smile at her (so close to a smirk) thinking of how her husband, small and wiry in the photo on her desk, would most likely fuck her. How, late at night and in the dark, he would like to think of himself as Napoleon, pushing her body into submission and fucking her from behind (with a receding hairline, on the back of a horse, with an army behind him ready to start the revolution). She stands up and gives me a key and a map of the caravan park. On the back of the map is a dot point list about how to use the washing machines, about how to use the detergent dispensers, the times when they're available for use. She turns her back to me, sits down and goes back to watching her television, laughs at the screen as Murphy Brown stands in a bar with Jim playing a piano – both drunk and singing 'Don't Get Around Much Anymore'. Simon walks me out into the morning sun. Past a group of drunk old men. Into the smell of garbage bins lined up and overflowing, and.

At the back of the lot, between the waste drain and a toilet block that smells of burnt plastic and chlorine, is my caravan. On bricks. With a worn yellow annexe. Simon nods towards a larger caravan across the path and tells me it's his, laughs and tells me he can keep an eye on me. I don't respond. He tells me that an old woman lived here before I did, that she had crystals hanging in the doorway, the smell of Camel cigarettes and dope always floating around her, her thick accent the first piece in the puzzle of her history. I am still silent and unlocking the door to the caravan, can smell her smokes in everything. He stands behind me and tells me that she would sit in an old canvas chair out the front of the caravan on weekends when the boys from work would get together and have barbeques (*What's better than meat fresh off the floor, bloodletting, your own doing, knife on the bone, knife tight up against the skin, eh?*), yell at them that the smell of burning meat reminded her of the dying mounds of humans she remembered from her foreign childhood. I look at my new home.

Simon brings my boxes from the ute and I stand beside him under the annexe, cursing him for his chivalry, lean in on him with my weight to show him that my body is made of gristle, as tough as the inedible tissue in meat. As tough as any man. As tough as him. Certainly, tough enough to carry some boxes. We stand together under the annexe leaning in on each other as the small specks of sun stream through the rips in the canvas and land on our skin. We step up. Move into the caravan. Stand together and look at its dirty grey lino floor, the brown veneer cupboards skirting the top of the walls, a fold-out red laminex table at one end and an old worn bed covered in a ripped plastic sheet at the other. Simon moves his hands to my elbows – moves me, moves in towards me as I reach up to open one of the cupboards. I tell him this isn't what I want from him. He grabs me and turns me to face him, moves his mouth to mine. (My body is made of gristle that can't be chewed through.) I push my breasts hard up against his chest and remind him quietly that I don't want this, that I am indeed my mother's daughter, and. He moves backwards, his mouth at the ready to kiss, to talk, to yell, to love, to hate. I don't know. I don't care. He tells me he will see me later, and walks across the path and into his own caravan.

That afternoon, I unpack my boxes and place the framed photo of Mallory and me on top of the small bar fridge. I look at myself in the long mirror beside the bed, see the squareness of my jaw, the tan lines on my shoulders, my hair wild and copper-gold-rusted steel, my shorts falling loose around my waist. I fold my shirts and my mother's underwear (why buy new pairs when hers are perfectly okay?), and place them on the shelves meant for tins of beans and cheap white bread. I pull my hair back into a fat bun on the top of my head and walk across the road to the pub, where I buy a carton of cheap wine and Marlboro cigarettes from a thin man with long greasy black hair. His hands shake as he passes me my change.

Back at the caravan, I sit in my annexe until the sun goes down, until the night sky is streaming through the canvas opening. I drink my wine from an old plastic cup I find at the bottom of the fridge, and know that Simon is watching me. I don't care. I open my legs and with my index finger slowly draw the outlines of the shadows of the moon onto my inner thighs and wonder what my mother is doing.

AT THE ABATTOIR THE MEN AND I ARE VIOLENT. Violent to the beasts, and. I wonder if the men are like this with their women. With their children. If someone will be like that with me one day – this place out here hushing fear and folding the echoes of wrongdoings under the cracking soil. I stand with the knife in my hand and watch the other workers around me; blood splashed on the bottom of their long white pants and caking in their skin, laughing with each other. A stab. A punch. A blow. The breaking, the butcher, the boning, the carving knife. Into eyes. (*Alive, dead, doesn't matter, Cynthia; they don't know what the fuck is going on. Dumb fucks.*) Into their ears. Chase it up the line if you have to. The young men's cocks hard with excitement. Break. A leg. A backbone. Slide off the skin in one go. Slow. Slow. One. Tragic. Blow. The sounds of, death. Forever, and. I find myself sometimes pushing my body up against a beast's hanging-heavy-weighted-pleasure for refuge. (There is safety in the small corner of the coldroom, skinned shoulders up against my chin. My body curving, my hips against the weight of hanging rump. Hold me.)

MOST DAYS AFTER WORK the boys and I drive up the road to Jerry's arcade. It's not far from the caravan park, right beside the local pool. We play air hockey, eat deep-fried food, sit in the back-corner booth and drink wine the owner sells to us in bottles. Girls younger than me (they come in after school, necks pale under the fluorescent lights) sit on the boys' laps, giggle at each other. Sometimes I feel Simon's hand on my leg and his wined breath at my ear. From time to time, a group of older men (skin olive-dark, hair oily with permanent waves) come into the arcade. I've never seen them around before, have no idea where they've come from. And they walk past us with their eyes low, with their hands in their tracksuit pockets, walk into the back office, look over their shoulders at me as they close and lock the door behind them.

ONE DAY, I'M SITTING IN THE BACK BOOTH drinking wine from a plastic cup with Simon, his best mate Cameron and a handful of other boys from work. (Silent. I've not spoken all afternoon. I've been thinking about the dreams I keep having of my mother. Of her calling the caravan park office looking for me. Of the woman in the office saying that her job description doesn't entail passing on messages to residents. Of my mother calling my name.) One of the older men, the one with the darkest skin, comes over to us, stares straight at me, raises his finger and points. *Come with me.* I don't say a word. The boys I'm sitting with, drunk and laughing at the thought of what these foreigners might want me for, slap me on the back as I get up. I push my breasts out (made of gristle from the toughest part of the beast) and stagger towards the office door, my mouth warm with wine and my work pants ripped and dragging on the dirty white floor. I stand at the door and listen as Simon tells me to come back. I don't. I enter the smoky room. Lamps in every corner. Glasses full of whisky, in. Their hands, on the tables, on the floor at their feet. Three men. A huge television with the sound turned down, showing a schoolgirl sucking on an enormous dick. Her head. Up and down, and up and down. The long shots showing that they're on a yacht and her left elbow has grazed to blood against the fibreglass that's flaking near the front seat. The men in the room all look up at me as I stand there watching the schoolgirl. They shift in their seats as a man with a lazy eye pours me a drink. I hear the groan of the man on the screen, watch as he slams into the schoolgirl's mouth, makes her swallow him whole. I'm watching as Jerry, the arcade owner, gets up and hands me a fist full of plastic-feel ten-dollar notes, points over to the oldest man sitting in the corner in an armchair. *This is my mate George, sweetheart.* Tells me that George wants to spend some time with me, that a hundred dollars is a lot of money for a young woman like me, that fucking is just plain fucking. *Make some money out of it while you're young enough to, darling.* Henry Lawson's face looks up at me from the palm of my hand, as Jerry leans in so close that I can feel the air from his nose on my forehead. He moves closer, the air between us thickening, and tells me that he knows who my mother was. And I don't move. Don't flinch. Don't move an inch, my throat constricting, closing, begging for fresh air. I look over at his friend George, who's slowly wiping his hands along the arms of the chair and looking at me. I fold my fist around old Henry's ten-dollar moustached face as George gets up and nods at me. I feel my breath release as I step back from Jerry, as I follow George towards the arcade's front door. One foot in front of the other. Look straight ahead. Don't make a sound. I feel all their eyes on me. I hear Simon call my name. Once. Twice. A young man sighing. *Whore,* one of them says. *Let her go. Just like her mother.* I keep walking. Outside. Sixty-eight steps to the old toilet block that's next to the local pool, and, how bad can this be for a hundred dollars, how bad can sex really be?

OUTSIDE, AND I'M under the sun that shines down on this town in a way I imagine people in other parts of this country would envy. My skin tingles, my skin warms, and I think of walking past the toilet block after a long summer day swimming with my sister. Its smell so piss-sour-strong from the heat that we held our breath and ran past it and into our father's waiting ute. *Whore. Let her go with him. She's just like her mother.* In the last toilet cubicle, I stand with my left hand in my pocket holding on to the notes. My head bows down to the dark cement as he closes the door behind us. A wife's homemade moussaka lunch on his breath. An overgrown and dying garden bed wild-sprouting as eyebrows. My chest out, and I am made of the unchewable parts between the ribs, the toughest bit on the beast. I grind my teeth until they ache. How bad can this really be? I hear a young boy laughing and running towards the pool. I feel George spinning me around, my head slamming into the corner of the cubicle. He's reaching around me, pulling my pants down, moving his cock into me (top limits high, dry soreness, his sound in my ear like a wild boar at an abandoned kill). I feel his hands rubbing up and down the sides of my curved, ready-to-burst-into-child-bearing hips. Pushing. My knees wide. The metal from the door's hinges making small indents in my forehead. His warmth inside me. (He, is the unpleasant surprise in a bite of meat, the bit you spit out in your hand when no one is watching.) *You feel just like your mother, you know. I always knew you were in the other room listening in on us.* He pulls out of me and pushes me towards the toilet's open bowl. I am on my knees. *Much more tender, though, love.* I turn and look up at him. He winks at me like this is the ending of a romantic comedy, leans down and kisses me. I want to ask him if, when he visited our home, did he think she was crazy?

WITH SMALL SPOTS OF BLOOD on my work boots I stumble into the afternoon sun; the street empty like the start of some western gunfight. I start walking home to the caravan park, stopping to buy a big bottle of Coke and a packet of salt-and-vinegar chips from the corner store, the treat my father used to buy us on weekends. I think of his large dry hands opening the bottle for my sister. The look on her face as the fizz touched her tongue. Her great delight.

THE NEXT WEEK, WHEN I WALK INTO THE BACK ROOM OF THE ARCADE, George hands me more ten-dollar notes – this time the paper ones that haven't been circulating for years. I follow him out to the toilet block and into the same cubicle. It smells of shit and bleach. As he fucks me from behind, I think of turning and punching him square on the jaw – a sign to him that I am just as dangerous as my mother. I don't. He slams my head into the back wall of the cubicle and whispers her name in my ear before he comes, tells me that girls like me are never believed. After he's finished, he leaves, whistling an old tune I guess is from his homeland, and. I pull my pants up and turn to see Simon standing at the metal handwash basin and looking at me. I push my hair behind my ears, feel a numb pleasure move through my body, become indifferent to everything around me and watch as he walks towards me. I flinch. I back up into the corner. He steps into the cubicle and reaches for me, pulls me out so that we are together beside the basin, so that the thin lines of light streaming through the holes in the bricks from the hot afternoon sun sit on our arms. He holds me and tells me that I could be beautiful. I smell the iron scent of his skin, the back end of the abattoir's industrial air conditioners in his shirt. I am as stiff as a board. And. I am not here with him. I am in some kind of moving memory. (For me, for you. When does memory start to fold in on itself, move, become our collective knowing? When does it become of every one them? Of touched, of. Taken. From behind, made me, you. Bleed. Told me, you to. Shut up, to call me, you Sir, Daddy, Buddy. Keep your, my head down. My, your, our jaws ache. And, folding, rolling out from large clenched fists. Taken out the back with your mates, your mates' mates, not your mates. Slapped. Pulled into. Cars, back stalls, you want the pay rise, right? Near that bonfire, a childhood bed, the back seat of your father's car, that wide brown land, coldrooms, your own bed, your, my head bashing up against the solid cold of a skinned hind leg. When?) Simon holds me. He tells me it will all be okay. I don't say a word. He tells me that he loves me, has loved me from the day we first met, and. I am silent.

We walk together out onto the street, and he pulls me closer as we see George's car slowly drive past us, his wife in the passenger side yelling at him, his hand slowly gliding around the steering wheel. Her blue-rinse hair, perfect. Bingo player – the type who is the first one to arrive on the day, pens in a line, feet solid on the ground, and. George lifts his head a little to laugh. Lifts his lips up in a half-kissing pout to me. His wife looks down at what I imagine are freshly manicured nails. I hold on to Simon's arm as we walk down the street, as he tells me that he will watch over me, he will be kind to me, give me a place to call home. I don't tell him that I want none of these things. I hear a car start in the next street. I can still taste George's tongue in my mouth as burning piles of old fallen wood, feel his skin pressed on mine as a young calf trying to stay alive, hung and moving past me in a closed room – a half leg kick and staring into my eyes for its liberation as it falls.

I DON'T GO BACK TO THE ARCADE AGAIN. On my way home from shifts at the abattoir, I drive past it without looking over at it. I imagine there is already some other girl walking behind George towards the toilet stalls, her eyes to the ground, her shoes dirty from riding her bike through the old creek beds that haven't seen water in her lifetime. I imagine the girl giving in to everything, wishing that she wasn't there.

I MAKE DINNERS ON MY SMALL GAS STOVE (stir-fried chicken, scrambled eggs, pancakes that I drench in chocolate sauce), bleach my work whites in a plastic bucket by the front door. I go to second-hand stores in the nearest large town about an hour away and buy clothes, books, old volumes of green leather-bound encyclopedias similar to the ones kept in a neat alphabetical line on the low bookcase in the hallway at home. (The full set given to my father by *a bloke who owed me a favour, love*, years before Mallory was born. *Bloody hell, Cynthia* – my father walking out from the toilet, doing up his zip with his left hand and the A–D volume in his right – *I know you love reading them, but can you just keep them in the bookcase in the hallway? Is that asking too bloody much?*) I stand leaning by the caravan door when Simon comes back from Sunday afternoon drinking sessions with the boys from work, and. He tells me one night, as he sways at the opening of my annexe, that the men out the back of the arcade now keep a double padlock on the office door, the silver keys hanging from chains on each of their necks. As I wait for Simon on these nights, the woman from the caravan park office watches me from behind her window with her arms crossed. I try to convince myself that she wants me. In fact, though, she hates everything I am – my face so much like my mother's, which was splashed across the front page of newspapers everywhere. I wave to her each time, and smile as she turns away from me to look at the television that's behind her.

SIMON BEGINS TO MAKE PLANS FOR US. He spends hours at the small fold-out laminex table in his caravan, hunched over the paper late into the night looking at the job ads. I see the light of his lamp still on as I lie in bed watching shows on an old black-and-white television he has bought me, reaching my leg out to move the coathanger that acts as an aerial. He brings over hot coffee in a big blue mug before work in the mornings and shows me lists of numbers and names that he plans to call in his lunchbreak, tells me he wants a local council job for the security and the better pay. *A man can't spend his life with his hands stuck in the guts of beasts, Cyn; a man's gotta move up in the world when he's got a girl to think of.* I sigh and half smile at him, remember that my father used to speak like this to my mother when I was younger, his excitement bouncing through the house like one of those rubber balls I used to dream of getting from the small vending machines in the corner of the bistro at the pub – all see-through, glittered and smooth. And, I wonder if my mother was silent with him like I am with Simon now.

Simon stays at my caravan on weekends, and we lie in bed watching reruns of *Hogan's Heroes*. He runs his fingers over my arms and presses his lips to my skin, climbs on top and we fuck without a sound – only a low groan when he's done. We walk to the corner store for fish and chips and smokes, and he tells me the names he'd like for our children. Looks down at his feet when I don't respond, when I light another smoke, start tapping my lighter on my knuckles. He doesn't ask me about what my mother did. Doesn't ask where my father might be. Standing in the caravan one afternoon, he moves his index finger around the edges of the picture frame on top of the fridge and asks about my sister. *Did she like sweets? Did she ever run away? Did she have a favourite toy?* I answer each of his questions about her, and. Simon tells me late that night, as we are drifting off to sleep together, his arms falling over my stomach, that he thinks that she is the only thing that makes me smile. He moves my head under his armpit for comfort as we drift off to sleep, as I hear him start to snore. I look over at Mallory and wonder, what kind of woman might she have grown into?

# I AM WOVEN INTO THE EARTH

THE WEEK AFTER I TURN SEVENTEEN, Simon gets offered a job at the council digging ditches and filling the potholes in the roads. I stand beside an old washing machine in the laundry as he tells me his good news, bend down to pick up a towel that's fallen from my basket, and remember my father's voice – *Another bloody pothole. Who do you have to fuck in this town to get a smooth ride into town?* – and my sister and I giggling beside him in the ute, not really knowing what the word fuck meant, except that it involved people naked and grunting and sweating. *Holiday pay. Long service leave. Bonuses at Christmas, Cyn.* Simon's voice brings me back to the smell of washing powder and concrete. *We can move out of this place and into our own house. It's all happening.*

He tries to pick me up and swing me around. He can't. *Jeez, you're getting heavy, Cyn. Time to lay off the chips, eh?* He laughs as he walks out of the laundry, and I hear him talking to the old couple who live in the caravan with the fake grass and knee-high picket fence around it, telling them about his good fortune, his plans for the future. The old woman calls out for me. She opens her arms wide as I walk towards her, hugs me, tells me it's all coming together.

Simon gives notice to the abattoir the next day, and before he leaves, the boys play practical jokes on him: leaving the dicks of dead beasts in his bag, leaving blades running near him that are supposed to be turned off. His best mate Cameron, who smells of salt and whose arms are scarred from his early days in the abattoir's cutting room, pulls me towards a huge bucket of blood. He lifts me up, holds me over it, telling Simon he'll throw me in unless Simon leaves a note for the boss on his desk with hand-drawn pictures of the boss's wife naked – *legs spread, the whole bloody show.* Simon laughs and tells him to do it himself, that he needs the holiday pay owing to him when he leaves, stands watching and laughing as I drop, as I taste the blood of a hundred slaughtered souls, shiver in their cold death. I rise up, my whole body dripping in disgrace, and. I push past both of them and go outside, hose myself down in the lowering afternoon sun. My body groans under the weight of being, and

I see Simon running towards me with a grin on his face. *Oh Cyn, love, it was all just a bit of fun.*

WE MOVE OUT OF THE CARAVAN PARK IN AUGUST. The day before the move, Simon's sister Michelle comes over to help pack. It's the first time we've met. Simon isn't here. He has a double shift at work; a cold snap has hit town, and potholes have started to pop up all over the place, the water beneath the road freezing and expanding. Michelle's skin is deep brown with the kind of tan that only women who have grown up on the land have; the kind that looks like it's inches deep, a scratch on the skin revealing only a deeper shade of brown. If she wasn't his sister, I think, she'd never come near me. She'd be the woman crossing her arms when I sat near her on a park bench, the one standing and shaking her head when she saw me walking down the street. *Walks just like her mother, doesn't she?* I put the radio on and turn it up, offer her a beer. I yell across the path to her as she's packing up Simon's caravan, when it's time for a smoke, and. We stand together under the sun as she tells me about the bands she loves, trying to make this all less awkward (Aerosmith, The Cure, some obscure punk rock band from the 70s that she promises me I'll get into once I take a listen.) We talk about things that don't matter, and I throw my smoke on the ground when I've finished, walk back into the caravan, start chucking out clothes that I'll probably never wear again. I yell across the path to her about the TV shows I love (*Heartbreak High, Neighbours – Karl Kennedy has just become the local GP –* and *Recovery* on the ABC, but only because I've got a crush on the host). *Oh, Dylan,* I hear her say to me with her head out the caravan's small window. The woman in the office stands and watches us, and I lean on the annexe door and smile at her. She shakes her head and turns her large body towards the postman, who's at her counter waiting with a handful of mail.

As Michelle and I walk into my caravan together to grab the last box, she stands close to me in the small space and runs her fingers over the gold photo frame that's now beside the bed. She smells of vinegar and moisturiser, her breath sour like off wine. *So this is your sister?* I nod and lean down to pick up the box at my feet. *Miranda . . . Miranda, right?* I shake my head. *No, her name is – was – Mallory.* She knows her name, I think to myself. Of course she does; everyone knows her name out here. I put the box down and lean past her to grab the frame, grab my Mallory, both of us together in the photo, sitting under a hose in green plastic buckets as our mother sits at a table nearby reading the paper and drinking from a stubbie of beer in an old Styrofoam holder. Mallory's wide mouth in the photo, her screaming joy. Her screaming, and. My face is a burnt flush thinking of her as Michelle moves in closer to me. *You do know Simon is the youngest in the family, right? All of us girls keep an eye out for him.* I don't move. I hold my breath for as long as I can. *All he's ever wanted was to find a good girl to settle down with and have kids — you know that, right?* I let the warm air slowly release out of my nose. She touches her index finger to the frame in my hand as I remember the water from the hose hitting Mallory's stomach, her patting her small hands into the mud to make the sound of drumming on the earth. She is drumming on the earth far away now, I think. *We know the kind of woman you are, Cynthia.* A beat. *If you fuck with him, we'll fuck with you, okay?* Her heavy young breath. *We are never going to be friends.* Another gulping of air as water from the hose splashes in Mallory's open mouth. *I'm only here today because of him. Not you.* Five quick gulps, one after the other, and. I don't say a word to her. I step back and listen for Mallory's beat on the earth, listen for her to push back a sound so booming loud in our ears that it helps Michelle to understand. I try to mouth words to her that will make her recognise me as a casualty in all this. I try. I lean down and pick up the box without saying a word. Mallory's fisted drum on the earth belongs in other places now, I think, as I walk out of the caravan with the photo frame on top of the box, reflecting the sun's light.

THE HOUSE THAT SIMON AND I MOVE INTO sits low-bricked on land that is wide and flat, and beyond its yellow-wheat tapestry of colour, the mountains in the distance are a soft blurring of grey reaching up to the pale blue sky. I imagine those flying over us, on the way to places I have only ever dreamt of, see our land as a small piece of a large puzzle, each piece a tone of parched hue, connected to the next, placed together with the hands of a strong-wristed God with patience and willed precision.

At the front door, Simon stands with a beer in his hand, watching me as I move a bench seat with my hips to a spot in front of our new bedroom window, its metal legs scraping lines of black into the old grey concrete beneath it. He walks past me and stands in the middle of the large gravel driveway in front of the house, the midday sun beating down on him. *It's a bloody nice spot here, Cyn, isn't it? I'm glad we spoke to the real estate when we did; don't reckon there's many houses outside of town to rent these days. Sorry it's not exactly what you were after, but at least we've got neighbours close enough, and the bench seat's a nice spot for you to read all those books you've been buying, isn't it?*

We can't see our neighbours. There is no human sound here; no cars, no sirens, no phones ringing. The land around us is wide and open, just like the land where my family home still sits vacant. Wide and open. A place where you can look out your kitchen windows, your front door, your bedroom window and see it all. Watch it. Feel the burning sensation on your skin.

The land as fire. Her little hands. Those screams. The pieces of the puzzle joined together – dark browns, light browns, dry yellow-white grass, large potholes, the roofs of cattle sheds and deep cracks in the hard ground. Each piece connected to the next until it reaches her, and now as a large circle of blackened land in front of my family home, like someone had dropped a lit smoke on their tapestry rug from above and let it burn all the way through, too stoned to notice it before it was too late. I need forgetting, I tell him, as he lifts his face and squints at the sky. He doesn't hear me. I tell him this again and again. I had told him already. I had told him as he looked at the newspaper, as he talked to the local real estate agent when we first drove out here to look at the place, fifteen minutes from town but nearly an hour away from my old home. A nowhere place, wherever that was, wherever that is, wherever it could be. I told him that I wanted sound, enclosed places, a nosy neighbour, a best friend who could pop around for coffee, trees in large groupings that held noise, moved noise, crashed down on bad men, on bad women, who bent the sounds of all around it. *Crazy, cuckoo Cyn. Watch out, babe, or you'll end up like your mother*, he had said with a smile on his face, a large grin, a smirk that told me he was just like the rest of them. I sit on the bench seat and stretch out my legs, push off my thongs and feel the heat of the sun soak into my skin, remember his confused face the afternoon before, when I met him at the front door after he had finished his double shift with tears in my eyes, wrapped in a heavy dressing-gown and unpacked boxes all around me.

SIMON WORKS LATE THROUGH THE SHORT WINTER and into spring, and I sit watching our new colour television each day after I've got home from the abattoir, waiting for him to return, with nothing but the sound of the possums playing chase on the roof or the cat we'd now claimed as our own meowing at the door to be let in. I take long baths. I drink tea and I think of Mallory. I become unhurried. My body becomes heavy and I sleep early and wake later than I used to, often racing to the ute without a shower to get to work. Some days we fuck as the heat of the oncoming day moves through the house. His sweat falling onto my chest. His eyes closed. That one final groan. I don't make a sound, and. I think to myself that this may be what people call settling down. (What is this idea that so many of you have, that we each need to settle, that there is a time to settle? What does settling bring us? What great joys beyond the boredom of being?) And I know it's not that for me, it's something else, something that I can't put my finger on yet. Maybe it's grief that is sitting unmovable in its immensity on my bones, or maybe it's my body storing energy for the next move, the next escape, the next place, wherever that is. I pour myself neat whiskies on these long nights when I am freshly bathed, when my skin is soft. I sit on the back patio and feel my feet cold on the concrete, look out over the old wire fence separating our land from the wide land beyond us – those hills dark and imposing, rising out to the next vista. I feel like I am woven into the earth as a thick red cotton, unable to pull free and move on, and. I sit at the glass-topped table with my legs apart for comfort, flipping through Simon's unread RACQ *Road Ahead* magazines that show me different places to visit across Australia, hoping to visit a hundred different cities, a hundred different towns, a hundred new highways in my lifetime. Places with tightly woven bushland, or cramped spaces, full of small rooms, crowded bars, trains where my arms brush yours, thin walls through which to hear my neighbour's late-night phone calls, the constant hum of a train line close by. The lingering smells of others' living. My senses are sharp, the smell of my own hands after smoking makes my stomach turn. I am always in bed and half asleep when Simon gets home, and I begin to turn my back on him at night when he tries to put his hand on my stomach. I start to notice wet marks under my full and heavy breasts each morning. I hold two hands under my skirt and place them between my legs on what must be the coldest night of the year and it brings me relief from the constant pressure that sits at my pelvis, and. I think I may know what my unhurrying is, what my body settling may be.

—

ON A RAINY SUNDAY, as Simon takes a nap out on the hammock that he has tied between two metal poles on the back patio, I jump in the HQ and take the fifteen-minute trip to the chemist in town, am given a 'talking to' by the grey-haired chemist about how not to get pregnant as I ask for a home pregnancy test (kept behind the counter, a way to make sure we keep all you women ashamed of your own bodies and what they are capable of), get a scowl and my change thrown on the counter from a woman who knows my mother's name.

I drive home and pull up in the gravel driveway, put the test down the front of my pants as I get out of the ute and walk through the front door. Simon is still out the back sleeping as I go to the bathroom, take the test from my waistband and pull my pants down. Sitting on the toilet, I rip open the pack with my teeth. I stop still as I hear Simon come in the back door and open the fridge, yell out to me, asking me if he has any beers left. *Top shelf on the left, Sime, behind the butter.* He grunts and closes the fridge door and goes back outside, turns on his radio and listens to the Sunday afternoon football – his team, the Tigers, are up two points up in the last five minutes, and he's back with the fridge door open and grabbing the next beer. I sit looking at the peach tiles on the floor, the cream wall tiles, the bath, the curved shower recess. I put the small rectangular test under my legs and start to piss as he yells at the radio for a missed goal, sit still holding the stick for what feels like ages, my fingers covered in my own piss, dripping into the toilet. I trace my eyes over the blue waved patterns of the row of tiles above the sink, count the number of little yellow-orange fish that are swimming across them all. Twelve. I realise I haven't shaved my legs in weeks, as I look down between my inner thighs, see the thick copper-gold-rusted hair going in all directions over my white skin and. Two lines. Two dark pink lines. I have no idea what that means, and I reach down to the packet on the floor and read the back of it, and, I realise there was a 'urine dropper' I should have used on the test. Piss is piss, I think to myself. Two lines are two lines. Pregnant is fuck. Is pregnant. (See your doctor for a more reliable result.) Pregnant. I put the test on the floor and get up, pull my pants up, flush the toilet, wash my hands, wipe them. I walk outside and I'm standing on the cold concrete beside him.

He's pacing on the patio with a smoke in his mouth as I stand with the test in my hand, the wrapper underneath it. *Give me two minutes, Cyn, we just might win this bloody match.* He offers me his packet of smokes and his lighter. Fuck it, I think, as I sit down on the green-and-white-cushioned chair and light one up, place the test and the wrapper on the table in front of me. He walks around in circles with his eyes on the radio. Thirty-three pacing steps and he cheers, a win. A win for his boys, and he sits down beside me with a beer in his hand and looks at the test on the table. He looks at me. He is starting to smile. He's looking at my left hand holding the smoke. I tell him I don't want a kid. He's getting up to take the smoke out of my hand. I tell him I will get an abortion. He tells me, as he takes the smoke, that he hopes it's a son, that girls don't fare to well in places like this. I tell him that this, this having children, isn't something I ever imagined I would do. He sits down beside me and tells me this is the happiest he has ever been, and I am feeling caught in his joy. I am a bear in a trap, a beast with its leg caught in the chute before it's shot, a mother thinking there is only one way out of this. A mother. My mother. No way out. From this. I sit still and don't say another word. He tells me I will be an excellent mother. His joy bounces off all the things that surround us; the back sheds, the old tractor near the fence, the boxing bag he hung up weeks ago but has never used, the glass back door, the fridge, the tiles on the floor in the kitchen, even the rusted milking tins left beside the driveway as decoration. He is a thousand rubbery glitter balls bouncing all around me – the lights in the house, the growing moonlight, the stars all reflecting his shine back onto my skin. He is a man of little else but this moment, I think to myself. As he ages he will look back on this as the moment that changed it all.

As we sit late into the night, I listen to all his plans for us. I tell him that maybe, if she is a girl, I will call her Ivy – like the plant that inches over the ground, that climbs trees and rocks and over walls and gates that might stop her from trying to move from place to place when she is older, flowering up towards the sun and following her own direction.

I SIT NIGHT AFTER NIGHT as my stomach grows, sucking on the nicotine Simon tries to no longer let me smoke and looking at the dishes sitting on the edge of the sink, breakfast cereal caked into them with the heat of the day's sun. In the last few months of my pregnancy, I've taken leave from work with the promise of a job when I return. The boss smirking when he assured me, knowing that women never come back to places like this, with its constant reminder of death, after they've had kids. My stomach grows. The skin stretches. I have cravings for chips, the sound of each bag opening making my mouth open in anticipation.

I tell Simon over and over again in these months that I'm scared I will do what my mother did. I tell him that I'm not a woman who is supposed to have a child. I tell him over and over again, and each time I do, he gets up and walks away. To another room, to the fridge (his head stuck deep in there looking for the chocolate he knows I hide from him), to the back door and out onto the patio to kick the boxing bag over and over again. Each kick a response to every word I say, and. I find myself alone and walking around the back of the house late at night, yelling out for Mallory in the dark, hoping for some response, some echo, for her to run to me from somewhere, anywhere, wherever that is. She doesn't come. She is long lost to the earth, I think. I call out her name again. I feel my feet grow numb in the cold grass. I stand out there for a very long time.

Simon tells me one morning, as we sit at the dining room table drinking black coffee and smoking (a scowl from him each time I inhale deeply), that he'd like to call our child Mike if it's a boy, the same name as his father and his father's father. I try to tell him that I'm not sure I'll make it through this. He laughs. I light another smoke. *Oh, Cyn, you've got baby brain already. Fuck, settle down with the dramatics.* After he leaves for work, I sit on the couch in the lounge room and watch an episode of *Sale of the Century* – Glenn Ridge who hosts it now is no match for Tony Barber. I sit and punch at my stomach as a buzzer each time I answer a question. In what country did bologna sausage originate? *Italy.* Which American president emancipated the slaves? *Lincoln.* A female bear and a female pig share what name? *A sow.* I punch harder each time I answer; some pleasure in an eventful win up against the suited contestants, some pleasure in hoping that it might rid me of this baby. (I am my mother's daughter.) I guess the Who Am I question correctly. (Born in 1958; first single was an international top-ten hit – 'Holiday'; dated New York artist Jean-Michel Basquiat.) *Madonna all the fucking way.* Pick the $25 on the Famous Faces board, Eddie McGuire's smarmy-rich-boy-fuck-him face turning in lights to reveal my win, and I get up and go to the kitchen, reach up to the cupboard above the fridge for the bottle of vodka. I take it back to the couch, sit with my legs spread and unscrew the lid, rest the bottle on my stomach and take a swig each time the word 'money' is said. I imagine Simon walking out and never coming back again, just like my father did. I imagine him lying still in another women's bed somewhere. I imagine him walking down the street and not knowing me. Not here, not there, but somewhere, and. Day turns into night as I sit, as I get up to piss too many times, hear a storm brewing not that far away, as I grab handfuls of salt-and-vinegar chips and eat each one slowly. I drink the vodka. I watch Tony Soprano on the television fuck a young Latino stripper in a back room full of smoke. I think of his large heavy body on top of me; his hands, soft from good living, around my neck; him walking away from me and never calling again; his inner anguish as his misunderstood beauty. My crotch starts to throb with the idea of him, and. I finish the bottle. I walk into our bedroom and put shoes on, a jacket, pull a scarf around my neck. I call a taxi. A flash of high beams twenty minutes later. A horn sounding, and. I'm in the back seat.

I'm winding down the window for air. I'm asking if I can smoke in his taxi. He's asking me where I want to go. He's driving for a long time. He's looking at me in his rear-view mirror. He's commenting on my hair. On the rain that's starting to fall. (*Thank fuck, eh, love?*) On a woman he once knew who had hair like mine. I look straight ahead and blow smoke towards him in the front seat. He knows who I am. He asks me if I want him to come back for me a bit later, saying that he needs the fare; it's been a slow day. The rain falls. *It's not even that bloody cold, is it, love, even though it's supposed to be bloody winter?* I give him five bucks and tell him to come back at ten.

And I'm out of the taxi and in the front door of the pub. Two young men are playing pool and five blokes in dirt-caked work gear sit in a line at the bar talking to the barmaid, who looks me up and down as I sit beside the oldest bloke and ask him if he'd like to buy me a drink. He does. He sits close to me. He tells me his name is Harry. I tell him mine. He touches my legs. I brush my hand over his crotch. I smell his salty scent and think of Tony Soprano grunting above me. I think of Tony fucking away his pain, of fucking away mine. Of the itch, the throb, the tingle, the want. Of the push, the pressure, the weight, the having. The numbing of everything that sat with me after George. That numbing. That dull. That stunned fog. (*Get back in there, Cyn, hit it one more time with the gun.*

*Its legs should drop. It won't even know what's happening. Cover its eyes with a rag if you have to.*) That space between feeling, between dropping, between it all beginning, ending, beginning, ending. That space.

Harry and I drink together for hours, my body languid, soft, agile. The rain has stopped now (it never lasts long here), and his teeth are a broken dull mess, as he tells me he's been working as a long-haul truck driver for longer than I've been alive, that he's got a daughter somewhere who's older than me. The young men playing pool order hot chips and gravy, laugh and rack up game after game. Harry takes my hand in his as the lights go up around us in the bar, as the barmaid starts folding the beer mats up while singing a song I don't know. We walk out the door, out the back, out behind the industrial bins; my chest twisting up against the cool metal as he fucks me from behind. I hurt, I bleed, I feel the baby kicking for release. The dull warm. The sodden. The gluey. He pulls away and taps me on my lower back, doesn't say a word as I turn and watch him walking away towards his truck, looking at his watch just as Tony Soprano would have. I am alone. I am pulling up my pants. I am lighting a smoke and watching the end of it – gold, red, alive up against the night. I see my mother's face beyond it, all sweaty-loved in our back bedroom, all crazy-struck-down-in-sadness-at-this-life-not-meant-for-her.

I put the end of the smoke on my left wrist, push it hard onto my skin and don't feel a thing. I see the lights of the taxi reflect on the still-wet road as it pulls up, and I walk over.

ON THE FIRST SATURDAY OF AUTUMN, in the last month of my pregnancy, I stand at the kitchen sink and watch a herd of cattle walking together beyond our property line, their path the same each time they pass by, the deep colour of the worn earth matching caramel bodies in the new sun. As I wash dishes, I hear Simon's parents and sisters arrive. I listen to Simon welcoming them at the door and push my stomach hard into the drawer handles that sit under the sink. I hold it there until I see them all walk in to greet me, feel the indent of the handle in my skin as his mother introduces herself and her husband, her three daughters. Michelle is their oldest, and she hands me a bowl full of salted nuts and pretzels. The other two, Sally and Britney, stand up against the wall not saying a word. None of them come near me; they don't move to touch my stomach, or hold me like I'm going to be a mother, to give them their grandchild, a niece or nephew. His mother stands near the fridge and crosses her arms, her disappointment sitting within the stream of sun that is covering her chest. It is sitting there for all of us to witness.

The parents, Colleen and Mike, have driven two hours from the city to visit us, picking up their girls from the nearest large town on the way. They have brought their own fold-up chairs and beers. Simon suggests they all take in the sun and the view on the back patio – *It's a bloody nice spot out here, makes you feel alive looking out over it all* – and his father rips a beer from the plastic rings and walks out the back door behind his son. Colleen stands for an awkward moment with the fold-up chairs under her right arm and waits for me, as the three girls move closer together like a swarm of bees near their mother. I grab a jug of lemon cordial from the fridge. *Rightio, let's go outside then*. I straighten up and place one hand behind my back for relief and walk out behind them, feel the soft breeze of the new season on my cheeks.

They all sit down on the fold-up chairs. I sit down (a heft, an expectant heft) on the green-and-white chair closest to the back door. Colleen asks about my cravings (chips, crispy chips, the crushed bits at the bottom of the packet the best, sitting between my teeth for hours after). Michelle asks if we know the sex of the baby yet (I feel her, she is there, she is forming within me – there must be a better place for her, a kinder womb than mine), and about my visits to the obstetrician (I don't have the heart to tell them that I've never once been). I sit still. I say little. I look down and twist my hair into tight coppered rings as Mike asks me if my father is excited to be a grandfather. *Sure, yep, he's really excited* – don't tell him that I've not heard from him since the night he left the house. That after it happened, there was three months of my father turning up once a week to the house with a box full of groceries and not saying a word to me. That since the night he left me, I'd only seen him once as I drove past the Criterion on the way to a shift at the abattoir. Had spotted him in the beer garden sitting across from Pat and his wife, a woman and young child with ice-blonde hair beside him – his white shirt and leather vest making him look like a man on a daytrip from the city. Simon moves in his chair with his head down, knowing there is no excited father-in-law around. *I reckon it's going to be a boy, Mum, I'm gonna name him after Dad.* She half smiles at him and then at me, knowing as I do, from their twenty years of unhappiness and separate beds, affairs and bruises, that I will never love him.

After they leave – his father half pissed but certain he can drive all the way home without a problem – Simon and I drive to the new shopping centre in town, which has a Bi-Lo, a fruit shop, a tobacconist and a shop that sells a whole lot of plastic things. My body feels like sour-heavy fruit. We get two packs of cigarettes, a crossword book for me, a loaf of bread, three extra-large bags of Smith's chips – salt and vinegar, cheese and onion, barbeque. I hold the bags in my arms as we walk back to the HQ, thinking of their flavours mixing together, each taste stuck between my teeth for later. A salt-crunch-pleasure, and. Across the road from the shopping centre is the old Chinese takeaway, Chong Ma's. *You want to get Chinese for dinner, Cyn, bit of a treat?* Simon asks me as he puts our shopping in the ute, looking over at me as I stand with the bags of chips in the middle of the car park. *Sure.* We cross the street, and as we reach the door to the restaurant Simon turns around to me and pulls both his eyelids with his index fingers – *Chrooong Maaaaaaaa's flied lice is good.* He's done this every time we've come here, and I tell him to *shhhh*, afraid that they will spit in our food or give us a smaller portion if they hear him making fun of them. We order (always special fried rice, honey chicken, sweet and sour pork, a big bag of prawn crackers, two cans of lemonade), then stand under the red paper lanterns with gold strings hanging from the ceiling. I sway my body from side to side as Simon sits down on an orange plastic chair and scrapes his fingers down the edges of a soy sauce bottle, tells me that having a family is the only thing he's ever wanted. I shift my weight from foot to foot and smile at him, his small thinking so contained, I think, so boxed up, packed, left in a garage for someone else to find after he has gone. I wonder why so much open space makes for such narrow thinking? *This land is not our friend*, I say to him. His brow furrows, confused at how these words connect to children and soy sauce and groceries. My insides feel like someone has pushed their fist deep inside of me, their fingers moving and expanding the organs inside (*just get your hands in their love, the thing's half dead anyway, it's been stunned a few times already, it's not gonna hurt you*). I feel a warmth run down my inner thighs, I feel her arms reaching up for my heart, I feel the terror in her breastbone pounding through my underwear as I stand up, feel my head lighten, look down to a pool of watery blood at my feet as our number is called. *Forty-five! Number forty-five, your order is ready.*

**THE ROAD THAT TAKES US TO THE HOSPITAL** that's just over an hour away is a long winding one. As we drive, I look out the window into the dark expanse but all I see is my own reflection, my skin pale and greasy. I hear Simon breathing deeply, his hands gripping hard on the steering wheel. I hear him scream out at the hospital that closed its emergency department years ago as we pass it. *It'll be fine, Cyn, women take hours to have babies.* I fade in and out of memory as we drive, hear him yell at me each time I fade out (stew on Sundays), reach over me (the bruises on my legs from when I tried to stop Mallory from climbing up ladders to our mother's back room), to put the window down and let the fresh night air hit my face (hit my face, Mallory's face, her darling young face, my mother's own face in the mirror late at night, crying at her madness; her face that night, staring out beyond those flames). I feel my girl Ivy lying across my stomach, feel her pushing down to block the blood and air to herself. (How did it feel for Mallory in her last moments? Does the heat of flames make you lose all feeling? Do you know you are dying?) I feel my girl's last kick, and I know before we get to the doors of the emergency room that she is gone.

I am picked up from the front seat by two large men and placed in a wheelchair. My arms hang over the sides and a rush of warm air hits me as the glass doors to the hospital slide open. I am being rushed past people sitting on joined-together plastic chairs. I am wheeled up a hallway and pushed through heavy swinging doors. I am lifted onto a bed where two nurses and a doctor stand over me – *Come on, sweetheart*, legs prised apart – I am sticky hot release. *Let's get you breathing properly, sweetheart, just a few deep breaths – you're in a bit of trouble here.* A nurse stands beside my head and massages my neck for comfort, and I feel a pin prick in my arm, feel that numbed-numb wanting move across my chest. Time moves slowly, and. The doctor stands with blue-crystal-thin gloves on in front of a heartbeat monitor. She can't be found in there, he tells me. She is not there. She is now someplace else. A nurse wheels over an IV stand as the doctor looks down at me and takes my hand. *Sweetheart, we're going to give you this medicine to make the baby come out.* I begin to fade out. *She isn't coming out alive, okay, love?* His voice trails off, and I listen for Mallory's voice to rise up to me as my own daughter's. A tube rises up from my arm. *Okay, sweetheart, let's get this little one out.* Three nurses, a pile of white sheets and a dozen plastic containers for syringes in my vision. One young woman collecting paper cups off the floor and my thighs showing sections of my translucent skin. There is no sound as my girl falls into the doctor's large hands.

As a nurse lifts her small still body to me – *Do you want to hold your little girl?* – I look away, shake my head – *No* – watch Simon's face fall, his foot on the floor loud-tapping his distress. The doctor puts his hands on my arm, says he's sorry, that there was nothing he could do. He walks from the room. A nurse wraps my girl tightly in a blue-and-white blanket and places her in a small cot near the window. I lie watching her. She is so very still, and. I am so very still and crying. I see Simon walk out behind the doctor, hear his fist slam on the wall of the hallway. He doesn't return.

METAL HITTING METAL. A CHAIR SCRAPING ON THE FLOOR. A women's voice telling me what time lunch will be served. *There's roast pork and veg on the menu today, love. Maybe some chocolate mousse, if you play your cards right.* I feel something cold on my chest, someone moving a blanket over my feet. I feel my body move towards Mallory, feel her breath on my face in our shared childhood bed, her hands holding on so tight to me, screaming, as my mother came for her, grabbed at her, bent her into unnatural shapes to try to silence her. I turn my head and watch a wardsman wheel another woman into the room, smell disinfectant, maybe blood. I begin to fade out and see my father standing in our lounge room, watching the three of us sitting on the couch together, a beer in his hand. I fade in again, hear the beeping sounds of a machine, and remember my father speaking to two men in suits underneath my bedroom window just after my sister was born, heard him tell them that my mother used to be so different, that he wasn't sure why she had started acting this way, that he had no idea why things had changed so quickly. He promised the two men that he would keep a watch over us kids, make sure we were okay. After they left, I heard my father open his gun box beneath the house, saw him walk out to where my mother's grouping of thinning horses stood eating hay, their manes silvery in the sun. I watched him shoot each one of them straight in the eye at point-blank range. Watched the horses drop around him, heard my mother's howls from the kitchen, and. I can hear a group of nurses in the corridor urging someone to take one more step. Hear them all clap and say, *Well done, darling, you did it.* I hear the woman in the bed across from me crying. She sounds like a small child. I feel my left arm drop as my eyes become heavy. I fall into heavy black.

# DEEP PATHS OF DESIRE

THE LANDSCAPE SURROUNDING US A COMPLICATION, OF. Colours, of. Tones, of. Deep furrows and soaring trees, bushes dead-heaving from the soil. Thin white clouds moving close to the tops of the blueing mountains. Grass once turning from emerald, to mint, to olive, to deepest black, now as a brittle-piss-gold beneath us as we walk across sunburnt paddocks. River systems, long ago fast-moving and carrying brilliant silver-shimmered fish all the way from me to her, now empty and moaning for rain from deep cracking beds of famine.

I wake up in the middle of what I think is a Sunday afternoon. I am given a paper cup of red cordial and a small plate of vegetables. I don't ask any of the nurses where they have taken my girl.

That night in the hospital, nearly a hundred kilometres from my family home – the place of beginnings and endings – the nurses sit hunched over their stations writing their daily reports. In my dark room, I get up and dress (someone has washed my clothes of Ivy's blood, and I wonder if my mother's clothes were washed when she was stripped down in a cell after her own daughter was found dead). I grab my purse. On the other side of the room I see the empty bed of the child-woman who was in here with me and wonder where she has gone, and. I walk out and down the wide corridor, catch the large lift down to the ground floor, walk out the same doors I came through days ago. No one looks at me, no one asks me where I am going, and. I walk out through the car park onto the main street, see the bright flickering lights of the service station next to the hospital.

At the service station I buy a cold can of Coke, see a shelf of barbeque chips displayed next to the counter. My stomach turns. I go to the back of the store and put my key card in the small cash machine, take out two fifty-dollar notes, catch my reflection in the windows as I turn to walk out, and see her – her wild copper-gold-rusted hair falling over her face, her square jaw firmly set, Mallory and I sitting in our father's ute waiting for her to bring us back ice cream or bubblegum. She lifts her hand to her eyes to scratch, to unblock, to move the image that she is certain can't be. We do this at the same time. We sit in this reflected space together, my mother and I, not here, not there, but somewhere – wherever that is. And, I hear the cashier in the store cough, point towards the door for me to leave. I walk out and stand and watch a truck full of cattle pull up for fuel, smell the beasts' fear, hear their confusion in the way they hit their bodies up against the metal enclosure, and I imagine Simon walking around in tight confused circles in our backyard, muttering the names of the dead.

OUTSIDE THE SERVICE STATION ARE FOUR MEN standing in a circle near their taxis drinking coffee from a shared thermos, their smoke rising around them. *Any of you want to take me out near the Thanes Creek?* I say to them. The one with a tattoo up his neck looks at me and walks to his taxi. *Get in, love – it's gonna cost you a bit.* I get in the back seat, give him the fifty-dollar notes and tell him to take me as far as the cash will get me.

We drive in silence out of town, until he turns on the radio to a talkback station and asks if I'm excited about the Olympics next year, tells me he used to be a bit of a sportsman himself back in the day, before his knee got smashed up in a car accident.

*Reckon I might see if I can get me and the missus some tickets to the opening ceremony, if I can. That would get me in the good books, wouldn't it, love?* I look out of the taxi window as the lights from the town start to disappear. The shades of the night against the land giving no clues to its nocturnal turnings. We drive through the next town, with the old hospital that Simon had cursed on the way in. We pass the abattoir, and then the house where I know Simon is now standing half pissed in a sea of his own tears on our back porch. We turn left past the racing club and drive the long winding road without streetlights to my family home, the sky above us opening up into bright stars.

We reach the front gate, the lights of the taxi showing it still locked with the heavy chain Simon had wrapped around the wooden gate post. The driver puts the car into neutral and tells me that the ride cost more than the hundred dollars I gave him, that he too has a younger sister. He hasn't seen her in years. He turns around with his arm on the seat beside him and says, *My daughter went to school with you in town, love. Janice – do you remember her? She moved to the big smoke about a year ago, works as an admin assistant for the Premier. Even got one of those fancy mobile phones for her job. I remember you were a bright young thing, weren't you? Won the regional spelling bee a few times, if I remember correctly.* I don't say a word, and remember that the year I turned thirteen was the year I started to understand that things were falling apart at home. Knew that we were different to the other families, to the other kids. I remember the bus ride home from school on the day that I decided I couldn't keep going there. *Hey, Carrot Top – why you look so weird?* I sat at the back of the bus with my nose in a book, pretending not to watch as the group of popular girls walked up the aisle towards me. *Move, Cynthia, this seat is reserved for us. Gosh, you're ugly. You don't even wash your clothes. Man, you smell.* I could feel my face turn a violent shade of red as I got up and moved to another seat. *Everyone hates you, Cynthia, everyone thinks you're a weirdo, you don't even talk in class,* and. I knew that I couldn't go back. Knew that the secrets that I held on to were ones they would never understand. *Cyn, love, best to keep things to yourself. We don't need anyone meddling in our family business now, do we?* (I am so very good at holding on to secrets, I think. Hold them all in. Hold them.) I knew that I didn't belong at school. *Cynthia, sit up straight and stop staring out the window. There is nothing for you to see out there. You are by far the brightest student in this class when you apply yourself. Pay attention or you'll end up working at the abattoir –* a line of boys in front of me in modern history class turning around and smirking as the teacher said this. My head weighed down with the shame of being so different. I knew that day it was the last time I'd take that bus, that. Mallory needed me at home, that. Any hopes I had of being something more than I was disappeared with each kilometre, each house, each property that the bus drove past on my way home. I knew that I'd be forgotten by all of them quickly. And I just didn't go back. When the school principal called I told him that my mother had decided to homeschool me. *No, she's not free to talk. No, she would not like you to visit.* Watched as he drove up the dirt driveway and walked up the front stairs, handed him a note written and signed by my mother. *Okay, Cyn, love, I'll write it as long as you promise to look after Mallory* – which I already was. And, I just stopped going, don't think my father even noticed, and if he did, he never asked why. He didn't ask much that year. So I became Mallory's mother. Safer that way, I thought. How wrong I was. I reach into my bag to take out money for the ride, and the taxi driver says, *Don't worry about the extra twenty bucks. Jeez love, you're probably the only girl from school left out here, they've all gone now, even the school closed down a few years back. Are you sure you'll be right out here on your own?* I tell him I'm fine. I get out of the taxi, reach into my pocket for the key to the padlock. The taxi driver flicks the high beams on for me as I bend down to undo the lock. I hear it click once, click twice, and I pull the half-ring out of the socket, let it fall to the ground. I wave to the taxi driver and yell to him that I'm fine, and he reverses and starts to drive away, beeping the horn as he disappears into the dark. I stand alone and listen for whatever the night holds (the heavy beating of the earth is a low rhythm).

I open the gates wide and pull a pile of pamphlets and envelopes from the letterbox my father made out of an old milk tin, put them in my bag and start to walk down the dirt driveway. Groups of trees on the mountain punch out like black fists towards the stars, the ground around me as a swelling curve. I have walked this track so many times before. When I was a young girl, my mother was always too tired or too angry to pick me up. I have walked around this last bend on my way home from school and seen our home with a sense of dread in my body, my heart racing. She was so often watching from the kitchen window, her hands in the hot soapy water. The moon, full and bright, sits above the house as I near it, reflects off the white bones of dead cattle that once must have tried to make their way towards the creek.

THE HOUSE IS JUST AS I REMEMBERED IT. It sits high on large stumps that are covered with white lattice, half painted and acting as flimsy walls beneath. The long and wide front verandah. The double garage to the left. The green-painted water tank to the right, the low fence around it falling down in places. Pot plants, now dead, hang from the verandah roof, put there by my father so many years ago for when my mother returned home from the hospital after giving birth to Mallory. I remember my mother didn't even look at them as she walked up the stairs and in the front door with the baby in her arms.

Before I reach the low gate, I see it. It's there. The spot where she died. It is indelible on the earth. Forever fixed there for all to see. I stand in it, am surrounded by it. I bend down and place my nose to the ground to try to find Mallory's smell – of baths after dinner, couch whispers, holding her late at night, fresh oranges from her open-mouthed eating, the salt water from her as she cried. She was still here somewhere in this harsh and undiscovered living. Out here, I think, the land was a culprit. Out here, so much between us – stretching along dirt roads and making deep paths of desire, reaching towards those faraway mountains, and sitting in the burden of the sweltering heat. I run my hands through the loose dirt and know that we will always be together. *This land holds secrets*, I remember hearing my mother muttering repeatedly at the kitchen sink in the year after Mallory was born.

I sit under the light of the moon and move my hands wider, start sweeping them around me, start to crawl through the dirt, place my fingers into every inch of it, let my face fall in the places where I am certain she is. I start building mounds of dirt around myself, dig deeper with my hands to find her. *I will go all the way to the other side of the Earth*, I say out loud to her beneath me. I sweep my hands in the deepest section of the dirt and find one of her small gold earrings, the one she got from our father on her fifth birthday. (Sponge cake with strawberries and fresh cream on top. Running around the house singing pop songs with Jessica and Stephanie, the daughters of my father's friend Pat, all of us in our pyjamas. A bowl full of fresh popcorn. A packet of Jaffas, our fingertips orange-red. My father sitting at the kitchen table smoking and my mother nowhere to be found.) I let the dirt fall from my palms and place the earring in my mouth, roll it around, let it hit the back of my teeth. I remember my father bending down low in this same spot, one hand bringing his rolled smoke to his mouth and the other grabbing handfuls of ash, letting it sift through his fingers, feeling for her. I remember watching him from the kitchen window, not knowing that soon he too would be gone.

I put the earring in my pocket (gold reflects moonlight, flickers as a darted glint onto the dirt, reminds me that this here is the beginning and ending of all things). I stand and walk up the stairs to the front door, lift my right leg to kick the door open and am aware of the bulky pad, still in my underwear from the hospital, moving. I feel the heat of my blood on my inner thigh, kick at the door. One, two, three heavy kicks. Drop my leg down and move the pad back into place, push the door with my left shoulder. (A body made for pushing, for holding, for taking the weight of it all.) Push it open, push. Push. One more, and the sound of breaking wood around the lock. Push.

Inside, I run my hands over the wood panels covering the lounge room wall and move towards the kitchen in the dark, trip over the plastic mat in front of the kitchen sink and feel the smooth surface of the fridge. Reach up to the top of it with my left hand and grab my father's emergency torch. It's exactly where I remembered it being, and I pop the handle up and wind the crank. Keep winding until there's light. See the dishes stacked after washing on the sink. Walk into our bedroom and see Mallory's clothes neatly ironed and placed on our shared bed. I pull open the white lace curtains, push open all the windows, let in breeze, let in moonlight. There's a box of long candles, some matches in the top drawer in the bathroom. I place the candles all around the house, light them, and think the land outside must be startled by our home's sudden awakening. I unlock the back door and push it open, walk out onto the back verandah and over to the steel box where my father kept his hammers and paintbrushes, nails, his oil for polishing the wood of the kitchen table. I open it and see the heavy boltcutter he would use on the wire fences; the same boltcutter I saw him holding early one morning at the lock on my mother's bedroom door (she stood beside him in her apricot satin nightdress, smoking, tapping her foot, her long slender body bored with it all, and his hands shaking as he looked at her without saying a word). I close the lid and walk back into the house and down the hallway to her room as small balls of grey dust swirl up from the floor into the air. My hands shake as my father's did that morning. My copper-gold-rusted hair falls over my shoulders like hers did. I stand and press the palm of my hand on the door to her bedroom, the lock she used long gone, and the boot mark still there from the night when the cop kicked it open. I push it slightly ajar and stand there in the soft light, and. Her room appears before me as shadows. I shine the torch in and see my mother's unmade single bed, the sheets pink with small yellow and silver birds skirting around their fraying edges. Above the bed is the long piece of fishing line hammered across the wall, and the hanging pieces of cut black ribbon that her sharp knives were once tied to. The torch light moves slowly across the cream-coloured wall, and I see the silver glint of the two knives the cops didn't take for some reason. Both cheap and thin – just perfect for getting in under the skin, I think. I move the light over them. They reflect kaleidoscopic memory over the walls in the room, and. The largest one has my father's name engraved on it in capital letters. I move the pad of my index finger over his name, move my fingers along to the small boning knife beside it, and I recognise it as the same type I use at work. (*Sharpen it, Cyn, hold it in a fist, glide it down between each rib.*) Around me are plastic flowers covered in dust, clothes she'd owned since she was my age hanging neatly on a long wooden rod. (Ladies, go to your wardrobe and take out all the clothes that you think you might fit into again one day. How do you feel when you look at all those clothes that you've kept for the last ten years? Do you hate yourself? Do you hate yourself for ageing, for your weight gain, for moving into new spaces with your body? What unmovable thinking was pushed on you by others? What a waste of your own wonderous energy. Now, pick up those clothes and throw them away. Give them to a charity, burn them in a bonfire – I will. Take off your bra as you do it, let those breasts of yours hang free.) There is a collection of small perfume bottles on an old uranium green plate and dream catchers crowding the window. I count them. There are seven. (If they catch your dreams, where do they collect together? Where do they go? I think of the other people that my mother's dreams may now belong to and hold my breath for the sadness that will come.) In the top drawer of her bedside table is a collection of condoms, of jellies and thin see-through underwear. There is a plastic pink-sequined purse full of twenty-dollar notes, and on a small shelf beside the window there is a framed picture of my mother as a young woman smiling and sitting on a swing. It is the only picture in the room. I take down the knife with my father's name on it and roll it around my fingers, wonder what great fear beyond this room made her become all this (scared of everything beyond these walls, her knives at the ready, those strange men walking down the corridor at night). I stand holding the knife and thinking of her, feel my body tense up with the motion of readying myself to bone the next animal in line, feel the urge to sink the knife into my thighs, into the tendons of my wrists. This. Feeling. This urgency to feel something other than this place, to feel outside of this place, this living, this homeland. Has. Not. Ever. Stopped. Since. That. Night, and. Skin torn, unloved loving, bruised thighs, of wanting to feel numb in the face of fearing everything, the call of the void forever sweeping and swooning around me, taunting as some reminder of my place in this vast land around me.

With the knife in my hand, I walk back through the kitchen to our bedroom, to the bed I shared with Mallory, grab one of her shirts from the pile on the bed and press it up against my nose (her smell doesn't exist anymore). I walk out into the lounge room. It's lit up like a funeral pyre. I reach into my bag and grab the pile of pamphlets and envelopes from the letterbox, sit down and spread them out across the floor. There are bills from the phone company. There are envelopes all of the same size, addressed to my father, to me, in my mother's handwriting, and. I start to open them with the blade of the knife, see that she has sent us cards. There's nothing written in them. They are blank. I think they are probably some kind of acceptance that we did exist together out here. Happy Christmas. Easter. Birthday. Birthday. Birthday. Anniversary. Cheap cardboard. Nothing.

Her probably believing that I was here waiting for each card to arrive, that I could forgive her, that my father was still here, not somewhere else. My mother probably thought that our lives went on together without her. They didn't.

With the torch in my hand, I go out the front door and head down the front stairs, walk under the house to the generator with the two large batteries that sit beside it. Kneeling down, I twist open the fuel cap, grab the jerrycan and pour what's left into the mouth of it. Push the red switch to *on*. Turn the fuel switch to *on*. Move the choke. Stand up with my foot on the edge of it. Pull the cord. One. Two. Three. On the fourth go it starts up. Release the cord. Step back. Hear the whirling sounds of its mechanics. Walk out into the yard and stand under the full moon. Alone out here. Alone. My mother's face peering out from the cop car. (The last time I saw her.) I stand remembering my father asking us where the knives in the house kept disappearing to. (Her slow decline.) I remember before Mallory was born, my mother's arms holding me in their safe confines. (Think of heavy blankets, of sleeping again as an adult in your small childhood bed, sheets tucked in all around you. Think of your lover holding you down and fucking you, all skin on skin, cheek on cheek. Think of your hands cosy in knitted gloves in winter.) I remember my father coming and going in those final years, standing and watching, bewildered as to what this had all become. I remember. Mallory's pale blue eyes. Ripped bedsheets. Pots thrown at walls. The land around us unresponsive to our collective undoing and descent into sadness. I remember. Copper-gold-rusted curls falling to my sister's small chin. Her favourite song sung under the covers as my mother fucked strange men in that back room. This land as fire, and. The sighing of faraway trees and clusters of dying shrubs as her body fell as ash into the ground. My mother thought we went on without her. We didn't.

I stand out under the moon until it starts to fade into a new day. Back inside, I let the candles burn bright, fill the bathtub with cold water, take off my clothes and look down and see the heavy pad, my underwear, my thighs covered in blood. I place my fingers between my legs and bring them to my face. I smell like the one-cent coins my father used to collect, like the moments after Simon and I fucked (always above me, our skin in a fiery-sticky concentration in those moments, me thinking that I could love him, that maybe this could all work out okay), like a clean metal kitchen sink. Each knife dipped in the soapy water. *Be careful not to cut yourself. Hold the handle as you take it out.* My mother's bloody hands.

My body slips into the water and I feel my skin pull in on itself, watch the water turn a light reddish brown. In the growing morning light, I sit as still as I can until the water looks like deep-red stained glass around me. Rest. I think of sharpening both the knives from my mother's room, putting them back in the kitchen drawers where they belong. I think of writing to her to let her know that my father, her husband, walked out on me and never came back. I think of throwing all her belongings out onto the land; burning it all, and forgetting her. I get out of the bath and grab a towel, see her old bathrobe hanging on the back of the door. Put it on. Walk around the house and blow out all the candles. Walk into my old bedroom, pull down the covers of our shared bed. I crawl in and try desperately to remember the feeling of Mallory beside me, huddled in to my chest as if it was the safest place she ever knew.

TWO DAYS LATER I walk the long road from home to collect the HQ and my clothes from the house where I had lived with Simon, hoping a car will pass that I can hitch a lift with, and cursing the fact that the phone line out here was cut off after I left (the reminders, the last reminder, the final reminder, the cut-off notice sitting unopened on the lounge room floor). I'm holding a water bottle and wearing a pair of my mother's old house pants and her boots, my father's favourite grey shirt, his wide-brimmed hat on my head keeping my hair and the midday sun at bay. I smell of the coconut oil my mother would put on her shoulders as she helped my father up in the top paddock. Around me the land is a handwoven rug of yellows that turn to orange-reds, pinks that move into browns and tans. Trees are scattered like tossed feed, each one standing alone and slowly dying.

The first car passes me when I'm about an hour out from home, and I stand and smile, put my thumb out and mutter under my breath, *Cunt*, when the driver passes me without slowing down. I keep walking and feel a blister starting to form on my right heel. Drink water. Listen as another car approaches from behind. Push my hair, just like my mother's – an entanglement of thick wire – under the hat (*Gosh, look at the three of you together, all that hair between you, you're all cut from the same cloth – bless*). I put my thumb out without looking back and hear it slow down, hear it beep its horn at me. I turn around, and. The taxi driver who brought me out here is smiling at me. *Fancy seeing you here, love. Had enough of that place already, have you?* I walk over and tell him I'm on my way to pick up some stuff from a place I used to live, ask him if he wouldn't mind giving me a lift if he's going back that way. *I'm a bit short on cash at the moment, I've had some time off work. Back soon, though, I hope,* I say. He smiles and motions for me to sit in the front seat. *No problems, love. Happy to help out. It's the least I can do for a young woman who's been through so much.* I get in the passenger seat and pull out my smokes, offer him one, light it for him when he nods. We smoke in silence till we get to the turn-off and I ask him to turn left, tell him it's about a fifteen-minute drive from here. *No problem, love, not that busy around here today, gives me something to do.* We don't speak again until he turns into the wide gravel driveway and pulls up outside the house. *Did you want me to wait here for you and give you a lift back to the farm, love?* he asks as I get out of the car. I tell him that I'm fine, that I've got my ute here, that I just need to go in and get a few things and then I'll be gone. It's okay, there's no one home.

I'm. Finding the HQ's keys in the fruit bowl. I'm. Pulling out a big red-white-and-blue-striped bag from the back of the bedroom cupboard. I'm. Filling it. Bras. Underwear. Jeans. Boots. Long-sleeved tops. Singlets. Deodorant. Hairbrush. Tracksuit pants. Unread books and the picture of Mallory in the gold frame from the bedside table. I walk out and put the bag in the ute, unplug the television and take it. Take one of the green-and-white chairs from around the back. Call the cat. Rattle a bag of nuts that's sitting on the bench. Nothing. I don't leave a note for Simon. I change into my work gear and place the keys to the house in the fruit bowl, walk out. I drive. To work. Eighteen minutes. Through the front gates of the abattoir, park the ute, and. I'm in the boss's office, his small windowless room full of papers and a computer that he never uses on his large desk. His fish tank full of bright yellow fish near the doorway, his over-weight body turning on his swivel chair that creaks. He looks me up and down and asks me if I am sure I'm ready to come back to work. He's heard the news. I look at him and say yes, tell him I'm ready, that he promised me he'd have a job waiting for me when I returned. Tell him I'm ready to start today, my stomach still bloated like that of a woman yet to give birth, my face as maddening loss in front of him. He sighs and looks down at his desk, tells me they need some extra hands in the boning and cutting shed.

I STAND AT THE METAL BENCH with my hair in a net and gloves on up to my elbows. The heavy apron hanging over my stomach is white. My long pants and oversized shirt are white – all pure white against the deep-death-red in this place. Above me, the platform is full of men grabbing at hanging carcases and slicing large knives down their torsos. Echoing all around us is the sound of bones cracking and fracturing. The cuts of meat fall onto the metal ramps that sit beside us, the beasts' heads dropping to a lower conveyor belt that takes them to the waste bin. There are thirty of us on either side of the platform, and I see Pat, my father's friend, standing above us. He moves around a hanging beast slowly, his hips nearly giving in after all the years of lifting beasts before the hanging conveyor belt was installed. His hands are as fast as those of the young men around him. He looks over to me and smiles. I smile back and move my wrist, my knife, through the gristle of a beast's shoulder, turn my head to the left when I hear three Asian women in the line giggling like children. I watch them struggle to push their knives deep into hind legs, try to rip skin and muscle open in one motion. I hear them talking to each other in their foreign tongue, watch as two of the men above us move over in front of the women and kick stomach and entrails at them, see it hit their chests. The women stop talking, stop giggling, and look straight at the men. I know those eyes, I think; those are the eyes of women who are standing in the place the world thinks they don't belong. And they are afraid of nothing.

Before lunch, a man I've only met once before walks up the line and stands beside me. He tells me the women had started working here a week after I left. *They only speak to each other*, he says. He tells me they are from Vietnam, that they live together in the old stockmen's quarters about half an hour's drive away, hang their work whites on the old wire gates in the early morning sun. *Drive past, love, and take a look. You can't miss it.* I take off my gloves as the lunch bell sounds, start walking out for a smoke and in the reflection of the metal freezer doors see the group of women walking behind me. I see them mimic my walk; their legs wide and stepping long, their hands in their pockets. I stop suddenly and turn around, see them all stop still, look at each other and then bend over laughing. I turn and keep walking out the side door to the car park.

In the midday sun I lean against the wall. Once painted white, the wall is now coated in deep orange-red dirt up to my waist, and above that it's covered in burn marks where we put our smokes out – none of us giving a fuck about what the building once must have looked like. The clouds sitting above me are like thrown feathers among the crystal blue, and. I am sure that there's nothing as perfectly placed as the sky above us all in this part of the world. I lift my smoke to my mouth and inhale deeply, exhale and blow the smoke up into the sky. I feel the heat of the sun on my chest, and watch from the corner of my eye as the Vietnamese women walk out, their heads pressed together and whispering. As they pass me they all turn at the same time and smile sweetly, then keep walking until they reach the concrete steps leading up to the toilet block. The smell coming from the block is old ingrained piss mixed with bleach and the lemon-scented handwash we use inside. The women seem not to notice or care about the smell as they arrange themselves on the steps, one above the next, their legs spread to cradle each other's backs. I take another drag of my smoke. I pretend that I don't notice as one pulls out a small metal tin of smokes and passes it around. They each take one and light up, exhale one after the other and stare straight at me. I reach my left hand behind my head and put the smoke out on the wall, throw the stub on the ground in front of me, and think that it's as good a time as any to go over and chat to them. Out here, I think, us women need to keep each other close. As I walk over to them, they all start laughing, stand up and move to the side except the one at the top of the stairs, who remains sitting. I see that she's got the foetus of a young calf pulled from its mother's stomach placed over her bloody groin. The other women start laughing and pointing from her to me. One of them starts to pat the sitting woman's head as she pretends to push it out like a child. She grunts, moans, then lets it drop to the floor and a woman stamps her boot on it, blood squirting up her legs. *Look, look, you, you big lady*, the sitting woman yells over to me. *All dropped out from you.* They high-five each other, press up against each other as a heaving swell of home-grown amusement, and. I stop in my tracks, turn away, shake my head and walk back through the side door, realising that everyone here knows everything about me.

That afternoon as we work, we all keep looking up at the large wall clock over near the sorting table. Together, we count the hours and minutes till knock-off time, and. I can feel the lies that Simon has told them all about me spreading through the shed – under the jute bag and between the two boxes of the wool press, sitting in the blood between the concrete floors and the anti-fatigue mats, under the conveyor belts, and held in the chambers of the vacuum machine. His fictions sit between the blunt edges of knives and their sharpening blocks, are coming up for air in the dip tank, and are in the extra kilos on the scales. Spreading, on. Lips, in. The backs of throats, out. Of mouths and glances my way.

The clock makes its last movement for us. The bell rings. We all walk out of the windowless shed and up the hallway to the washroom, take off our aprons, boots, hose away the smell of death as we stand over the grates talking. I lean over the basin scrubbing my arms as the bloke beside me gets naked and steps into one of the showers lining the wall. There's no room for gendered pleasantries in here I think, as I sense someone standing too close to me, turn and see Simon's friend Cameron, smell his salty skin mixing with the bleach and lemon. He smiles at me as he scrubs under his nails with a heavy brush. My body is a tight-veined muscle, my nails digging so deep into the palms of my hands that I am certain I have broken the skin. He moves closer. (He is a salty lake in summer.) He says to me under his breath, *I know what kind of woman you are. We all do.* I scrub the deep, dry crevices between my fingers. *That baby wasn't even his, was it, Cyn?* I stop scrubbing. *We all know you've got a taste for the old fellas, right? Eh?* He winks at me. I reach for the old hand towel hanging on a rack above us and start to wipe my hands. *We all know what happened that night at the hospital, some other fella turning up with a bunch of natives. You sly cunt. You never thought Simon would find out, did ya?* I bend down to pick up my boots. I don't say a word. *You're just like that slag of a mother of yours.* (He knew, all of them knew about my mother before they knew me, the whole country did, her infamous deed spread over every front page and news report the week she did it, the words *Baby Killer Slut* spray-painted on the road out the front of our property.) *No bloody wonder your father took off for something better.* I walk over to the lockers and open mine up, pull out a clean pair of socks and walk with my boots in my hands over to the bench. Cameron follows and sits down beside me. *Fuck off, mate*, I say. He puts his hand on the seat, touching my thigh slightly with his pinkie finger, and snorts through his nose. *We know the whole story, Cyn.* He moves his face close to mine. His stale breath sits on my lips as he pushes his fingers deep into my thigh.

IT HAPPENS OVER SLOW MONTHS. The boys at work who were once my friends, who sat with me and Simon at Jerry's arcade drinking vodka, start to brush past me in the walkway between the boning and cutting shed and the packing shed, start to make excuses to come by when they know I'll be on a shift. They stand behind me making small grunting noises. They draw pictures of cocks on scraps of paper and slide them into my locker.

They push me up against boxes in the storeroom and follow me outside when I go to smoke, standing so close to me that I feel my jaw start to ache with tension. The Vietnamese women giggle and watch on, their newly learnt word *whore* coming out of their mouths. Their bodies moving closely together. Their shiny black hair tangling as one. Their pink-gummed-taunting, together, reminding me of a pack of rats whose tails' get caught in a gummy mess and are unable to survive for long – an omen, a sign of a looming plague.

On a Friday afternoon when the heat is starting to come alive on the metal roof of the shed (a canopy of creaking metal, stretching and bathing itself under the new season's sun), and the women-who-are-afraid-of-nothing have all gone outside for an afternoon smoke, I walk to the fridge in the tearoom, open it and grab the plastic bag of testicles they have collected to take home and cook up as soup. I walk over to the bin near the punch clock and throw it in, look at all the time cards on the wall stand in front of me, search for the female names among them – find them: Thuy, Maggie and Kim. I pull each of their cards from the stand, punch them in the machine one by one. All three finished for the day, and not even knowing.

—

TO GET AWAY FROM THEM ALL, I start to take my smoke breaks down at the two old unused sheds that sit behind the holding pens. The beasts in the pens blink wide-eyed at me as I walk past them. I watch their bodies push up against each other for a piece of shade under the roof next to the ramp that leads to the chute and to the kill floor inside. An old bloke with leathered skin who never speaks to anyone stands among them with flies gathering around his mouth. He moves the beasts along by pulling and twisting their tails, and pushing a large and bloody stick into their eyes when the beasts freeze with fear. Those cattle closest to him lift their hoofs up and down, make low guttural noises. They know what's coming, I think; they know that they are about to die piece by piece in there, and. They piss and shit all over the ground, their chemical smell moving beyond the abattoir and all through the town, gag-inducing in the summer months. The line keeps moving, the next beast falls through the chute and is now caught in a box and stunned with a bolt gun to the head, is shackled by the hind leg and moved to the slaughtering shed floor. (*Lift it, lift, stick it, stick the throat, bleed that fucker out, that's it, get him good. Oh, this one's a tough fucker. Stick it. I reckon some are bound to believe they are fucking immortal hanging there with their hoofs kicking. Just how it is, eh. They'll die eventually. Just let it hang there till it does. My hot tip: don't look the bloody thing in the eyes.*)

The two sheds I'm standing behind were used to dry and salt sheepskins before they renovated the place over a decade ago – all numbered and loaded up, tied down on the lorry and driven all the way to Sydney. The sheds' green corrugated-iron walls are now half falling down and rusted, and an old square wool press still sits concreted into the floor inside. I can hear the beasts' grieved wailing rolling low over the land, can see the men from the kill floor who were on the early shift, leaving for the day, walking to the car park and hopping in their cars. Start them up. A wave. Music on. Forget the day. Put the air conditioner on full bore so the expensive air freshener their wives bought them is the only thing they can smell (they all know, like I do, that the smell of death is a linger, a meld, a deep swallow). I lean on a corrugated-iron wall and light a smoke, slowly inhale, slowly exhale, look out at the crowded bushland beyond me.

The bushland behind the old sheds is different to the rest of the land out here. So dense, with a wild spectrum of colour unlike anything I've ever seen before. Arcs of vivid light from the sun bounce between clusters of bushes and rocks. Brilliant beams blaze across the uneven ground that's carpeted in layers of maple-brown and green fallen leaves, finding places to rest and allowing me to see sections of the bushland celebrated in mottled light; then leaping towards large clusters of olive-green native grass, jumping towards blooming soft wattle trees growing thick, the weight of their fragrant yellow blooms bending their branches towards the ground as if each part of the bushland is tending to the next. So contained and realised in this space, an arrangement of soft welcome for those who notice it, and. So unlike anything else in this part of the world. The forever parched and brown-red land beyond this involved space, for generations, surrendering to the oppressive heat and shortage of rain. *Hotter than a shearer's armpit, as sticky as the resin from a bloodwood gum, sweetheart,* my father would say as he walked in the front door, taking his long-sleeved shirt off and sitting at the dining table in his wet-all-the-way-through blue singlet, sweat pouring from his temples. I can hear magpies, honeyeaters, the mobbed and clamorous living of small animals that I imagine are in there. The soft-wind swaying of ironbarks and stringybarks. I imagine, green tree snakes moving through the trees, their graceful sliding motions; green frogs, their skin a wet minty glow, waiting on the edges of light to catch bugs and insects; grasshoppers in groups, the males rubbing their legs against their wings to create great symphonies for the females. Right here, in front of me, on this patch of land no bigger than our property at home, and. I wonder if it knows of its own strange importance in this tale. Wonder why it has been knowingly ignored by all that live in this part of the world, ignored by me too until now. I inhale deeply, feel smoke scratch the back of my throat, and.

Remember sitting in the ute between my mother and father in the abattoir's front car park one afternoon, my mother having promised to pick him up from work on our way home from shopping for my new school shoes in town. I remember him pointing out this bushland to me – *See it, love, out the back there? See all the colour?* – and telling me that the old blokes who worked on the killing floor with him thought that the reason it was so green, so teeming with difference, was because the blood, piss and shit from the cattle that flowed into the long grates and underground pipes must have ended up out there. All that blood and bone had made this a place of unlikely abundance among the dry. *Just shows you, sweetheart*, my father said as my mother drove the ute out of the car park and towards home, *that from death comes life, from life comes death. It's a circle, love, just like how the seasons keep rolling around us.*

Each lunchtime behind those sheds, a pack of smokes hidden under an upturned coffee tin and sitting on a metal chair, I lean with my back against the rusted walls and feel the sun on my face. I watch the colours bend and play in the bushland in front of me, take off my plastic boots, full of blood and bits of stretched animal skin, and peel off my wet socks (one day I find the small ear of a calf and hope it's a sign of good luck). I stretch out my legs and look out to the tops of the river red gums reaching up from the bushland and swaying in the hot breeze, feel them bending towards me from their wet-soiled base. That they even exist here makes me think that a river probably ran right through here once, that the trees thrived along its banks, and. They seem to reach closer each time the hot wind brings them my way. I feel as though they are watching over me, comforting me from where they are, fixed in the lush-heavy-layered-maze of evergreen shrubs and orchids, ferns anchored to tall pines, climbing vines forever reaching for the canopy of bunya and hoop pines, over groundcover moss, large hunks of quartzed granite, pebbles, small dark rocks, fallen branches. This is a place that should only exist in places of high and regular rainfall. This place is an aberration, an act of defiance against the world around itself. I sit before it. I am fixed like never before. I sit. I am. Safe here. I feel my chest expand like an exalted martyr's would towards whatever is before her. In this place, here I am.

Where the abattoir's land ends and the bushland begins, the ground is marked like a child's painting – the deep dry brown-red of hard-packed dirt giving way to a carpet of leaves, to a vivid rising of involved colour. I get up, I walk to stand on the edge of it, turn to look back a few hundred metres to the abattoir beyond the old sheds, see a truck loading cattle into the holding pen to the right of it, and the two water tanks beside it, each filled every fortnight from tankers that have driven the water to us from the city since the dam level dropped under twenty per cent, the lowest in eight years. (The abattoir was awarded 'water relief' by the state government because it was 'an essential business for the survival of our economy', and. Two days later, wire fences were built around the tanks to stop the locals from siphoning water out for their stock.) Straight in front of me are the stained walls of the largest shed, the small frosted windows belonging to the toilets and the changing rooms inside. To the right of that is the back door, where two men stand and smoke. And past them is a glimpse of the car park. Each day out here there are new sensations – the leaves breaking under my feet at the edge of the bushland, small pieces of gravel pressing in on the pads of my feet and between my toes, dense honey myrtle shrubs scattered around the bush's edges reaching out for the sun and brushing against my hands. (*They call this honey myrtle Revolution Gold, love. Good for wind breaks. Go on, grab some, it'll be gone soon with this dry. Throw it up in the air and see all the flecks of gold floating around you.*)

Finally, one lunch time I stand beside two river red gums reaching straight up to the sky, their bark a smooth cream colour with patches of yellow and pink. There must be hundreds of them in here, I think. There must be thousands of other kinds of trees and bushes in here. I recognise the emu bush, with its soft grey leaves and brilliant red tubular flowers, from a photo my father showed me in one of the encyclopedias (he and I always showing each other new things from them, pages dirty with thumb marks and constant turning); huge bunches of soft-to-touch maidenhairs that I know my mother would have given her left arm for; so many others that I don't know the names of, that I have only seen near death and unrecognisable on our property at home – shrubs and plants my mother probably knew growing up as a young child. A gentle hum beneath it all. A soft rustle. A building symphony. A tropical composition of grand proportions. Wet ground, soft and so foreign, sticks to my feet and I feel the beating sound of life, the. Beat, the. Rhythm, the. Hum. The softest breath surrounding me. I walk up to a birch tree and press my mouth up against a small hole on its trunk surrounded by sap. I whisper Mallory's name into it. Whisper again to make sure her name reaches the smallest circle, the tree's first year of living – *Mallory*. I wait for the beat, the breath of her. I wait for her hum, as all around me the ground vibrates with what I'm certain is the soft stamping of a thousand women around me.

EVERY DAY AS I LEAVE WORK, I see a group of men finished for the day, talking and smoking in the car park. They all stop and look over at me as I drive past them. One holds his cock with his full fist through his dirty white pants, his groin moving up towards me. Two brothers, a decade or more apart, place two fingers at the edges of their mouths and push their tongues up and down between them. They do this every day, and. I watch the mouths of the other men. Words like *fuck* and *cum* and *suck* and *slut* roll out over their lips. As my ute nears them, I imagine putting my foot on the accelerator and mowing them down like a drunk young man who sees a snake in the middle of the road as he's driving home from the pub with his mates. I imagine throwing buckets full of chemicals at them then flicking a lit smoke. I don't. I won't. I am not my mother. One afternoon, I slow the car and roll down my window, smile (like a good woman should) and hoick the phlegm in the back of my throat, spit it right at them.

ON MY NINETEETH BIRTHDAY my name is listed on the tearoom corkboard with some streamers and a thirty-dollar gift voucher for drinks at the pub – the one in town that belongs to the owners of the abattoir. The one with a bar made out of an old bit of oak, cold XXXX on tap and a karaoke night each week ('Khe Sanh', 'Horses', 'You're the Voice' – *Come on, just play it, man*). The streamers have been used again and again, and the voucher looks just like the one my father used to get every year. (I remember hearing my mother complaining to my father on his birthday when she was pregnant with Mallory that the only reason he even got a birthday gift from the abattoir was that they knew they would all use them at the Christmas party at the pub each year. *Just putting money back into their own pockets, the tight fucks. Seriously, love, it'd be better if they actually bought you lot down there some new steel gloves. I'm sick of seeing you come home with bloody cuts all over your hands.*)

As I unpin my voucher from the corkboard, Cameron (salted salty salt) walks in behind me and asks me to help him with a half beast that has fallen from the hooks in the coldroom, tells me that he needs all the help he can get to heave it back up there. I stuff the voucher in my bra (good for holding so many things: a set of keys to grab and poke him in the eye, a razor blade sewn into a small pocket for those moments when shit just gets out of hand. Contrary to popular belief, ladies, your breasts are your greatest line of defence). *No. Fuck right off, mate, I'm not going anywhere with you*, I say, and he raises his ungloved hands in surrender, blood streaming down to his elbows and dripping on the floor. One of Simon's other mates walks past the door of the tearoom as we are standing together. *It's all hands on deck in there – better get a move on, you two. Cyn, the boss says you're strong enough to help us out, says you better get your arse in there as well.* I look at Cameron and sigh up at the roof. *Fucking hell.* Follow him to the coldroom.

—

IN THE COLDROOM the air swirls around me. There are rows of half and full beasts hanging against the farthest wall. There are stainless steel benches and the sound of Cameron whistling behind me, the vague presence of others lingering behind a towering pallet load of already packed rump. I move around in a slow tight circle, looking for the fallen beast. It isn't there. One of the men behind the packed rump clears his throat. I hear another one say that they only have five minutes before Pat gets back from his tea break. My breath changes to short gasps. I know what this is. Cameron grabs me, presses his bloody elbows onto my shoulders, pushes me to my knees. I tell him no. I tell him. Stop. *Stop.* I tell him, *Don't.* He unzips his pants, places his hands around my head. His knees push into my breasts, and. Faster. Faster. Back and forth (salt builds up in the ocean). Forward. Back. I close my eyes to pretend this isn't happening. *Mate, move to the side and show us her face, will you?* I hear one of them say my name. Their voices are moving closer. I hear my own wet muffle, my own gagging, feel Cameron's warmth down the back of my throat. My head hangs. I. Can't. Breathe, and. There are now three men, perhaps four that are close. A grouping of blood stained work boots surrounding me. A haze. My hands fall to my sides. Do I hear my fingernails breaking in this cold? *Fuck, she's a slut just like her mother, all right. Could probably take a couple of us, you know.* I feel my body lifting, my hair pulling at my skull, the stinging chill of the coldroom's stainless bench. My breasts pressed flat. A ripping – the loudest sound I can imagine. Packing tape across my mouth. I tell myself to try to remember the voices behind me: the pitch, the range, the tone – am sure I must know at least one of them. I can only see metal, focus on a small scratch mark from a knife in front of my face, feel a hand on the back of my head, a warm dick inside me. My body goes limp, and. The sounds of Mallory are now all around me, echoing from the land beyond. Loud. Louder. Running all the way through dried creek beds and over fallen logs, across the bones of cows once plump for slaughter, over roads travelled by women to find refuge, past hospitals now condemned, over the chests of women waiting in fright and waiting in line for their turn, thousands of women before her/me/us who never made it. She is coming all the way to me. Mallory. Her little feet red with earth-wanting-angered heat. She stops the sound of moving air. She is rattling the air-conditioner pipes that run across the ceiling above us. Shaking. A break. The largest pipe cracks open just above the men, falls on them, one large heavy section after the other. They all jump, step away from me, yell at each other to get the fuck out. I hear Pat coughing up a lung as he walks past the coldroom door and shuffles up the walkway, back from his break. And each man, a. Zip, a. Cough, a. Slap on the back.

Cameron's deep laughter. A huddle of feet moving away (what is the collective noun for a group of men like this – a terror, a calamity, a butchery? A butchery). I pull up my pants. Move one foot in front of the other. Steps. Too many to count.

# A EULOGY OF COLLECTIVE LOSS

I WALK FROM THE abattoir's back doors until I am leaning against the rusted green of the back sheds. (No one sees me here. I am invisible up against the green metal and rough surface. Airbrushed. Legs angled to show the slimmest section. My gut heaving inwards to stop the pain. Jaw up to the sun, lips pouted and grabbing at air just like a thousand other women in magazine images.) My stomach is an aching cramp. My breasts are the throbbing of an oncoming bruise. My knees are an iced numb. I light a smoke and sit down, pull my pant legs up over my knees, flick the lighter again and move the flame over the cold raw skin to thaw it out. I feel like I'm about to vomit. I am sour smell. I am last night's dinner. I am hard-metal recollection. I look up and out into the bushland in front of me and know that I am beyond this place, beyond this kind of living.

I swallow heavy, feel small chunks of last night's bread sit at the back of my throat. And. I. Rise, my copper-gold-rusted hair wild with electricity, and walk into the bush, hold my breath in and listen for the sound of silence to break as I move past the hanging wattle. Listen for, the echo, the murmur, the whisper. Listen for Mallory, hear her voice, her sweet sound. I walk further, until I can no longer see the abattoir. I take off my boots, my apron, look up to the river red gums that have grown so strong and tall in this place forever, take in their lemon scent, and. Remember before Mallory was born, remember my mother and father sharing the master bedroom, the back bedroom full of boxes of my mother's half-finished craft projects, my father sawing into a large fallen tree and showing me the rings as its lived years. *One hundred years, sweetheart. Imagine what it's seen out here.* My mother and father's laughter in the evenings as they played poker and drank home-brewed beer. And, I wonder if the fallow land that surrounded us knew what was to come? I begin to hear a beat around me that matches the pounding of my own heart, feel it as the soft embrace of other women, feel the heat of their living in the base of my feet. I sit down in the dirt and with one hand start to build small mounds of dirt around me. Gather nearly dry leaves and build the mounds to castles, light each one around me and pass my arms over the tops of the flames, a rich blaze, my skin bright brilliant and aching for their living sound.

AT FIRST THEY WHISPER. At first, they are a cooling breath on my shoulders, are the waving fronds of a tree fern higher than me. It's so much cooler in here than in the outside world, and. I sit hugging my shoulders, blow my warm breath on my hands. Their whispers rise as I look all around me. Their whispers become chitchat, become conversation, are voices heard on a soapbox. First, there is a group of sisters: they never had a chance in the small room they were kept in. Then there are other voices rising into oration: a woman named Lynne, drowned nearly one hundred and fifty years ago in the river that used to run right through here, her bones found by dogs months after he killed her. Then Margaret, whose uncle often crept into her bedroom late at night – how did her mother not know? Then there is loud-talk, yelling, the sound of feet stamping on wet leaves; just one punch to the back of the head was all it took to kill Christine. And, all around me there is loud screaming anger in the tallest trees (*toughen up, love, take it*). Louder (*no jobs for women here. You can't lift like the men, can you now?*). Pressing on my skin as a known sermon (*how many times do I have to fucking tell you?*). Each word a layer. Each voice a eulogy of collective loss (*yeah, mate, she takes it from behind like a dog*). The small flames around me are now the sound of wailing women – or is it young children? I can't seem to make out which. And, I hear her. I hear her. I hear Mallory's voice among them, hear her whispering her favourite ice-cream flavour in my ear, feel the cool sensation of straight-from-the-freezer-you-can't-have-any-of-mine strawberry sherbet on my tongue. She says my name. I hold my breath. My cheeks swell up and blush with the thought of her, with the thought of all our collective misplacement now here together. Our voices bouncing off the roots of a large spurwood, racing along large hunks of granite and folding into each other. Our sound together here, I think, in this crowded place, is a revolution.

TWO

# THIS IS THE HOUSE

THIS IS THE HOUSE of longing, of. The building of our shared grief, of. Our mother's displacement. This is the house that is now hard-set on the land from years of drought, from welcomed torrential rains, its wooden stumps now bonded in the hardest red and brown earth, and kilometres away from anyone. And, this is the house that Mallory was killed in, has escaped. I sit on the once-white wooden front steps and smoke, feel the near-midday sun sting the tops of my feet. I pick the skin from around my toes and let the smoke hang from my mouth, look out at the large patches of red dirt and bursts of dry yellow grass surrounding the house, the dirt driveway, the green corrugated-iron roof of the neighbour's house – just visible on the next property. This is the house that has a hallway, that has a phone sitting above a bookcase full of green leather-bound encyclopedias that I once read cover to cover, over and over. This is where I stood with my bare feet on the wooden floors this morning and opened the small black book, flipped through the pages until I reached the letter T – *Timm Brothers' Meats*. A number I'd known all my life but could never memorise. (I remember my father wrote it on a small piece of paper and sticky-taped it to the fridge the year Mallory turned two – *just in case your mother doesn't feel well and you need me.* I laugh out loud thinking of this. He knew all along it would end badly.) This is the house that has the hallway that has the phone on which I called the number this morning. *I need some time off. Yep, a week probably.* A sigh, a grunt, a *fucking women, should never bloody give you jobs,* from the boss. *No pay for casuals like you,* and. *I can't promise there'll be work when you get back, Cynthia.*

THIS IS THE HOUSE of shelter now. My body bruised and sore. The place I can bathe, stretch my legs and move my head from side to side to release the tension in my neck. I get up and walk along the hallway, feet bare on the cool wooden floors, run my hands over the tongue-and-groove walls. Beside the low bookcase there's a silky oak desk that has always held notepads and pens, old screws, light bulbs, sticky tape – things that my mother probably thought would come in handy one day. I take out a notepad, a pen, a cream envelope. *Your husband walked out and never came back. The ashes of your daughter sit in the earth.* I write these sentences again and again until I have filled a page. Then I rip it from the pad and fold it, place it in the envelope, write her name in slow-motion-thick-cursive on the front. I tell myself that I will drive to the post office in town and put a stamp on it, post it to her at Baillie Henderson, the hospital for the mad and the insane – once called an asylum. (I won't.)

I go to the toilet to piss, walk into the bathroom and undress, turn the shower on and stand under the red-hot-burn-my-skin water, swallow the heat to soothe my aching mouth, feel the skin where the hair was torn from my head. I draw crude symbols on the fogged glass with my index finger – love hearts, my initials – like I did as a child. When the water runs cold, I grab a towel and dry off, wrap it around me and walk back into the kitchen to make a cup of tea. I reach up and lift the lid off the old tin emblazoned with big orange flowers that sits on the shelf above the oven, its pattern matching the smaller tins beside it that once held sugar and coffee. (*Your grandmother used to love baking sponge cakes, Cyn – the smell of them always reminds me of her.*) There's still a handful of teabags in there and I grab one and hold it to my nose. It's only got the faintest smell to it now. As I'm about to put it in a cup, it drops to the floor. I bend down to grab it and feel the sweat run from my temples to the tip of my nose, stop a moment to look at my reflection in the oven's glass door, stained brown from age (my nose, my eye pits, my full set of teeth, smell my sour breath). As my sweat drips to the floor I see my mother's reflection as my own, hear her clear her throat as I do, see beyond my image to my mother's bedroom behind me. The door wide open. The reflection of her bed, a pair of slippers under it and, pushed back further into the shadows, what looks like a box. I get up, put the teabag on the bench and, forgetting the cup of tea, walk into her bedroom, drop down to my hands and knees, lower myself onto my tender stomach and reach under the bed with my right hand. Feel for it. Touch it. Grab it. Wooden. Hard. Cool to touch. Pull it out. It's about the same size as the toolbox my father used to keep in the back of the ute. A crack of my knees as I stand up. A throbbing between my bruised thighs as I walk with it back out to the lounge room.

I sit on the floor, leaning against the couch, and open it, place one hand in and feel paper – the glossy, scratchy, thickly, thinly, largely, the small. Feel piles of it. Grab at it in fistfuls and put it on the floor beside me. Keep grabbing. The pile rising. More of it, and. There's a black-and-white photo of a young couple and a child, with what looks like our house behind them – but the land is so lush and green surrounding them, that at first I don't recognise it. Gazing at the image, I listen for the women's voices that I know are around me somewhere. I can't hear them.

There is another photo. This one shows my mother and my father on their wedding day, his chest out proud and her eyes focused on something in the distance. Her dress is long and white, and my father holds a can of beer in his hand as she sits on his lap. I return to the box. There are two locks of hair – mine and Mallory's from when we were first born, copper-gold-rusted hair (*so much of it, darlin', a bloody shock*) tied with faded pink ribbon – and my mother's parents' death certificates stapled to a newspaper article. Killed in a car accident on the long stretch of road right near where Thuy, Maggie and Kim now live. No witnesses. Found in a ditch on the side of the road days later. Their bodies ripped apart by wild animals.

> Local cattle farmer Henry Davies and his wife, home seam-stress and church volunteer Joan, originally from Liverpool, will be greatly missed by the local community.

A misstep on the land, they said. A sad loss for their only child, my mother, who was sent to live with a distant relative in the city. The picture in the newspaper is the same as the photo I'd just found of the young couple and a child in front of this house. At the bottom of the box there are gold rings, a folded-up piece of blue material. I sift through the paper on the floor, the glossy, the scratchy, the thickly, thinly, largely, the small. Hand-drawn maps in bright colours. Pictures cut out from magazines of trains, libraries, convenience stores, movie cinemas, offices – places full of the echoes and mosaiced murmurings of other women, I think. More photos (some black and white, others in colour – my mother, her hair as copper-gold-rusted as mine and Mallory's, holding the two of us, our hair tangled in the wind as one booming firestorm). I find receipts dated from around the time my mother and father met: restaurants and movies in the city. A Greyhound bus ticket stub with BRISBANE stamped on it slipped inside a Valentine's Day card showing a love heart with fire blazing around it. The message *Forever burning for you, my lovin' wife* is written inside, and under it my father has drawn a picture of my mother with her hand on her stomach, and an arrow pointing at it, and. I know that at the end of that arrow, in her stomach, is me. This is my beginning. Our bond, in this brittle old card, in a box under her bed, in this house, on this land – our beginnings, and. There's a cover ripped from a paperback book that has a picture of four young black women holding hands under the title *The Colour Purple*, and a quote written in deep blue ink that says: 'Whenever you trying to pray, and man plop himself on the other end of it, tell him to git lost, say Shug. Conjure up the flowers, wind, water, a big rock.' I imagine my mother sitting alone in the back bedroom and trying to conjure up flowers and wind and rocks with the quiet stillness sitting around her, as my father is becoming someone else, somehow swallowed up by this place and unable to resurface for her. The promise of their wild love quickly disappearing, her long days at home alone watching for him to return. Dinner cooked and placed on the dining room table. His, head down and eating. His, eyes half closed. Her, asking him about his day. There wasn't much to tell her, as the rains finally hit that year when I turned six, when great sheets of water moved across the top paddock, when the silvery beacons of eucalyptus trees fell from lightning that cracked open the grey-blue howling sky. (You have been tricked for years to think of your/your best friend's/my mother's, my father's land, as your companion, as a place where romance builds, where futures prosper, where the great Australian colonial dream unfolds – a weekend away camping to make memories, a jutting rock as a shaded picnic spot for morning tea on Valentine's Day with your school friends as a lovely outing.) I wonder if she had asked my father when they would leave for other places. Her heart a slower beat as he left her each morning, I think. The curtains drawn, the coffee sitting hot in the kitchen brewing, and the sound of his ute driving away. My mother had told me once that, before I was born, she'd be out on the property helping my father – fixing the wire fences, branding, recording calving dates and weights of the stock. But it never was her kind of thing. My father had wanted to run four hundred cows, like her father once had; he thought that the wet decades before were bound to continue. And, she got bored of the land after a few years, pretended that she was ill, had housework to do or craft projects that would make them cash. Endless days of walking the paddocks and watching herds of cattle in the distance cluster around shrinking patches of green brought her no joy. After I was born, my father surprised her with a new black-and-white television, and she'd watch shows about women at work, women at bars, best friends talking about husbands and lovers, women beaten and raped in New York City. She watched them all, she said, until one day the TV signal just stopped working, didn't reach their house anymore. She never bothered to ask my father to fix it until around the time I started walking. *Needed to get it fixed then to keep you still and bloody entertained, love, 'cause that big brain of yours just never turns off, does it? Turned out a possum had snapped the antenna. An easy fix, your father said.* But in the time the TV wasn't working, the silence became eerie out here, she said – *bloody eerie, Cyn, like there was something brewing.* She started reading the local newspaper left in our letterbox at the front gate. *Educate myself a bit better with reading and all that. Your father loves the papers, always has. Supposed I could learn to love them too.* She walked up the dirt path to get it each Wednesday, would read every inch of it, attempt the crossword puzzle before my father could get to it, even wrote a few letters to the editor about the rising cost of smokes and the abattoir starting to hire people from out of town, from overseas, instead of the local blokes who needed the work. *Your father was furious at me for writing that one. Thought they'd recognise my name and give him the sack for it. Of course, they bloody didn't, did they?* She told me that when she first read about Lindy Chamberlain and her baby daughter who was taken by a dingo, she felt like she had found a kindred spirit. All that red dirt surrounding her. Her voice heard all over television stations and in sound bites on the radio. Her, innocence. Her, guilt. Her, voice an echo, a beat, a sage-vibration to all the other women across Australia, as she stood with those large sunglasses on and her son in her arms. *I just yelled out, 'Has anyone got a torch? The dingo's got my baby.'* I run my hands through the papers beneath me and find the front page of the newspaper: AZARIA: PARENTS BOTH GUILTY is the headline above photos of Lindy driving away in her car and her husband Michael being walked out of court with a detective holding his arm. The date on the newspaper is from 1982, and. My mother has drawn a red heart around the picture of Lindy and a line racing down the page to a map of an upgrade of the North Australian rail line. Perhaps, I think, this was my mother's way of saying to me: *Get out while you can.* Little did she and my father know, my mother said, that the big drought was about to hit, that interest rates were soon to go through the roof, that everything had changed for good. I close the lid of the box and turn it upside down, see that she has sticky-taped to it a folded-up piece of paper with my name written on it in frantic handwriting.

THIS IS THE HOUSE in which, when I was ten, Mallory was born. This is the lounge room where I remember my father holding her, her small just-born hands reaching up for rays of sunlight, trying to catch dust and things that the adult eye could never see. *Sum, sum, come sum*, were her first words, were a revelation to him that morning so many years ago. Her voice still sounds in this house, on this land; still moves up the hallway and in under the covers with me; sits still in dusk – that wondrous thin place where day turns into night, a soft pinkish haze rolling over the land. She is in the reds of the blooming bottlebrush at the front gate that just won't give in to the heat, and in the tufts of brilliant green grass scattered over the hard red ground. I open my mouth and roll her name over my tongue as I carefully peel the sticky tape off the box and hold the folded paper in my hand. Her name now sits in the same spot as her first words did. A place where I don't belong anymore, a place where we should never have been in the first place. *You. Don't. Belong. Here.* Back then, our mother began yelling at the walls, started loud-stomping down the hallway, and. I remember that after she'd moved all her things into the back bedroom, I'd lie in bed thinking that she had somehow become fixed, anchored like a ship in an ocean, to this house – her locked bedroom door a dead giveaway. I wondered, did my mother know something we didn't? Did she know something more? I wondered if she could hear more out here than her own beating heart? My father started leaving us around then, on his motorbike up towards the top paddock, in his ute for days at a time, and. I remember that my mother didn't blink an eye when I told her that I had seen a pair of yellow high heels in the front passenger side of the HQ. Turned away from me when I said it again. They were such a strange thing to see thrown in against the black rubber on the ute's floor, their shock-shining yellow coming from another place, not from here – but from somewhere, wherever that was, wherever that could be. I remember that the morning before I told her, I had waited for him to get on his motorbike and head to the top paddock, raced down and opened the passenger-side door. I reached in and moved my index finger softly over the shoes, saw the ashtray in the door pulled half open, menthol cigarette butts with bright pink lipstick on their ends sticking out. I knew right then where my father went, and. I remember that I grabbed one of the cigarette butts and put it in my pocket, slammed the ute door shut and raced up stairs to my bedroom with it. I'm not sure what I did with that cigarette, but I knew that my near-silent father, already somewhere else, was gradually forgetting us; that we were just his stop along the way to something better. He was a man who didn't know how to deal with it, a man who found his future in something else. This is the house that my father walked away from without a goodbye, leaving me behind, just months after that night, the night when it happened; his hat left on the gate stump and the ute out the front of the house with the keys still in the ignition.

—

I MOVE BACK OUT ONTO THE VERANDAH and sit on the front steps with the note from my mother in my hands. I know what it is that I'm about to read. The sun has lowered into the western horizon and I think of the good times before Mallory was born – my father's heavy feet running to my room to scoop me up on the weekends, the sizzled sound of him cooking steak in the kitchen, the radio playing classic hits – pop, The Beatles, the sound of English summers and Australian new modern living. A slap on my mother's backside as she walked past. Giggles, and. Her laughter so bold-bright in those years. The sound of his wheated-beer breath in my ear when he told me that he loved me. And, here I am, still in this house and sitting in a young girl's remembering of how it used to be. As the sun sets, I begin to hear the faint sounds of women who never made it, swinging and lolling on the branches of a large hanging plant at the lounge room window. Singing softly, to. Mallory, to my grandmother, to all those women before me placed somewhere they didn't belong. To, those out of place, out of time. Those, forgotten. *Come. Find us.* This house. This. Bonded together. All of us. Our history. Out here, each one connected to the next, and to the next, running across the earth. And, I am crying. There is no going back, I think. There is no one left here now but me.

# HE WAS SOMETHING, CYN

GERMANY IN JANUARY FOR BEERS AND PORK KNUCKLE. You know, I once watched a program on the telly about the history of it breaking in two. Then off to Rome in February – all water and rubble. Did you know that the Vatican is a city within Rome? A city within a city – how bloody weird is that? Off to Spain for two months after that. I really wanted to see the bullfighting. Blood sport, they call it – your grandfather used to say that it wasn't sport, it was just an act of desperate men. Whatever that meant. The plan was for your father and I to then go to Portugal in May. To sit on the water's edge and drink good coffee, eat all those tarts everyone always raves about. Do you reckon the Portuguese call their tarts Portuguese tarts or just tarts? Gotta wonder, eh? You know, I would have made a bloody excellent matador.

I MET YOUR FATHER two years after I came back out here. It was so bloody quiet living alone in this house. And so hot. So still. Why the hell your grandparents never put ventilation in the place when they built it, I'll never know. I used to sit on the front steps and watch the heat swirling up off the land. It always looked like a weird oily ghost or something. I'd sit with sweat rolling down my back and wish for rain that never came. It's been so dry out here for so long, love. Too long for us to hold out hope anymore. But your father did have big dreams when he first came here. The next farmer on the land, well-fed cattle, rolling pastures or something like that. He spent weeks fixing up your grandfather's tractor and the fences (well, we both know that fences always need to be bloody fixed, don't we, love? An ongoing job). He even got a farmhand in to help him put a new roof on the cattle shed. The trees that used to give off so much shade just didn't do the trick anymore.

Bloody harsh land. So bloody quiet. How do people do it and stay happy and sane? When I was first out here alone there was nothing to do but the weekly run in to get groceries and talk to the locals. I remember there were a few old birds from the CWA who'd opened up a room on the side of the church that was both an op shop and a craft shop. Should still be there. The one next to the town hall. They sold coloured paper and glitter in those thin clear tubes. Big bottles of Clag glue. They'd get the stuff delivered from the city once a fortnight and would always sell out of everything before the next delivery was due. When I first went in there, one of the old women, Narelle, remembered me from when I was young, talked to me about your grandmother, how she used to be in a sewing circle with her. She made me a cup of milky tea and gave me a fresh scone with jam and cream, told me how my mother used to help out at all the church functions, that her wedding was a bit controversial due to her being pregnant. *Not the kind of thing a young woman did around here*, Narelle said to me. Before I left, the women gave me a Tupperware container full of jam drops and a box full of craft stuff. Even threw in some stickers for fun; said to me, *They're really for the kids, but we love them too.*

FOUR DAYS AFTER MY EIGHTEENTH BIRTHDAY. That was when I came back here. I arrived on this doorstep in the early hours of the evening after being on a bus for five hours, after hitching a ride from town partway and then walking the rest. I had to jump over the locked gate. I was bloody exhausted when I finally reached the top of the steps and took my boots off. And all I had with me was my backpack with some clothes and a hairbrush in it, and the letter from my parents' lawyers.

The letter had arrived a few weeks beforehand, telling me that my parents had left me the house and a whole whack of cash in their will for when I turned eighteen. And you know, Cyn, I'd never even thought about coming back here until then, never thought that there'd be money waiting for me. I'd been living such a different life in the city for so long. Taken there in the back of a cop car after the accident, I guess. I couldn't remember it. Too bloody young and confused probably. I only remember standing with the two cops at the doorstep of a man called Richard who was related to my father. He was an older bloke who'd moved to Brisbane from England a few years before my parents died. He'd never even met my dad, Richard told us as we stood there. He had no idea what to do with a young girl. He shook his head and walked back inside when the cops told him that I had nowhere else to go. Didn't say much to me that night as I hovered around the door to the lounge room wondering where to put my backpack or if I could sit down. He was a bloody mean man, Cyn, that Richard. Beat up his girlfriends and only talked to me when he wanted to be fed. My only friend back then was the cat he let me get. Smoky I called it. The little thing slept with me on a mattress in a back room of his house (well, it wasn't a room really, more like a closed-in verandah – sloped ceiling and twenty-three windows that would rip open with the bloody westerlies), until one day it just didn't come home. I guess it got run over or went to another house where it felt more bloody welcome. You know, the old bastard didn't even send me to school, said education was for boys, that women belonged in the kitchen. What a cunt, eh?

Coming back on that bus here, what I remember most is the loss of sound along the way. It scared me shitless, love. The city's loudness turned into a hum when we hit the suburbs and then, the farther away we got, it turned into this softer sound. When I finally got here, it was all silent. Cyn, do you remember that night in the bottom paddock when we both screamed into the distance, hoping that the night or the sky or the trees or bloody *something* would recognise us out here? Hoping the land would tell us that, yes, we were a part of it just like everything else out here? Do you, Cyn? Do you remember me laughing and bending down to you as you got pissed off waiting to hear something? I looked you straight in the eye that night and told you that I had done this exact same thing the night I first came back here. (I stamped and screamed, punched my hands into the ground to make some noise. To hear something other than my own breath. Nothing. Nothing. Bloody nothing.) Remember what I said to you, love? Remember? *Don't wait for the sound to come back, darling; I don't think it ever will.*

—

THE POINT I'M TRYING TO MAKE, Cyn, is that I was so alone out here in this house. And I got so bloody bored of staring at the walls and trying to work out what to do. You know, though, I really took to the crafting. Really took to it. I loved making cards with sayings on them (the more glitter the better), hand-made picture books with heaps of colour in them. You know, love, I reckon in another life I would have been an artist. Might even have made some money out of it. There's only so many things you can make, though, before the pointlessness of it all gets to you, I suppose. So, I taught myself to drive your grand-father's car, learnt how to check the engine oil, the brake fluid, the coolant. Took me a while, but I even taught myself how to drain the petrol tank to get that thing started again. It drove like a dream till your father ran it into that bloody statue of the old premier from the 1800s – that Roman Catholic bloke who sits smack-bang in the middle of the intersection in the main street in town. No cuts to your father, mind you, but a bloody sore head the next morning from the booze.

At the end of that first year out here, I had started to make the long drive back into the city to find some people my own age to talk to. Don't get me wrong, love – people out here like a chat, but it's all gossip about everyone else. And, well, after your parents get killed in a car accident, it's the only bloody thing anyone in town wants to talk to you about. For fuck's sake, it was bloody years ago. It's not like I even really remembered much about them. Another reason for going was that it always seemed to be so bloody hot out here. So much unmoving heat. And I'd think these weird things, Cyn, as I got closer to the city. Like, the wind was the open mouths of women blowing a breeze. That there weren't many of us women out this way and that was why it was always so bloody still. So, anyway, I'd make sure there was enough fuel in the tank and check the air pressure in the tyres, pack a blanket and pillow so I could have a few drinks and crash in the car at night. I always wore my mother's high heels. Really, really bloody unfashionable those things were, but I mean if I've got enough red lipstick on no one's going to be looking at my feet, right? Red. Red. Red. Red hair. Red dress. Red lips. Rose perfume that I'd found in the top of Mum's wardrobe, on the back of my neck. And I'd even put a bit of foundation on, but it would always drip down my bloody neck. All the bloody time. I'd have to spend another ten minutes putting it back on when I got to the city. I'd always go to the same bar. I met your father there, you know?

THE NIGHT I MET HIM, I was sitting and drinking a Bundy and Coke in the public bar of the Regatta Hotel. I was looking out at the huge jacaranda tree that had probably been there since the place first opened and feeling the breeze from the Brisbane River moving all around me. Gosh, Cyn, it was so bloody nice there. The colour of that tree, a cold Bundy and the brown river racing past. I reckon you can't beat it. You really need to make sure you get there one day, if you can. I sat there, the only woman in the public bar, thinking about those two women who had chained their ankles to the bar rail demanding a beer in the sixties. Cyn, love, I'm not sure I agree with all this women's lib stuff going around these days, but I tell you what, those women are bloody champions in my eyes. A woman deserves to sit and have a cold drink in any goddamn place she likes, I reckon.

That night, the women sitting with their husbands and kids in the lounge opposite kept looking over at me, and I sat staring straight back at them, I did. I pushed my tits up high so the men around me took more notice. Just for a bit of fun of course – stupid bloody women not understanding that those other two fought for me to sit in here without their stupid glares. I remember that the pub smelt like that old cement in public toilets. You know, that musty, dry kind of smell it gets from years of pissing and fucking and fighting. I ordered another Bundy, and at about seven o'clock I saw another woman come into the public bar. She had this pitch-black hair and long legs, real exotic-like, with these long thin hands, and she stood at the other end of the bar from me. All the men looked at her and I heard one of them say she looked like an elegant bird. Fuck me, Cyn, it's like these fuckers always have to call us women something we aren't, don't they? So, anyway, a guy walked up beside her and bought her a drink, sat down with her and pushed his hands between her thighs. Right there in front of everyone. He handed her fifty bucks and they both walked off to the toilets together. You'll find this funny, Cyn – there wasn't even a chicks' toilet in there, just a blokes' one. Things change, eh? And I looked over and saw those women who were sitting in the lounge were now looking at the toilet door, waiting for it to open up again. Their husbands and kids kept eating their meals, and I kept drinking my Bundy, and then I heard a guy behind me ask if I'd like to play pool with him.

I stood up, full of Dutch courage, and walked over and grabbed the pool cue out of the wall stand. He laughed as I walked back with it and handed it to him. And then he asked me where I was from. And I told him. I told him that I felt like I didn't belong here, or even there really. I felt like I was always in a nowhere place – wherever that was or whatever that bloody was. Then I asked where he was from. And this guy – your father, Cyn – he told me that he wasn't sure where he belonged either, that all he knew was that his father had come out here on a ship from England after his mother died. Knew that his old man had dropped him off at a farm with two old farmers. That he remembered the killing of sheep one after the other when they needed money. He didn't know much more than that and guessed he wasn't from anywhere. Probably didn't belong here or there either. He laughed after he said that, and his hand reached for mine as we sat and drank our Bundys. He was something, Cyn. He was something.

Sitting there that night and playing games of pool, your father made me feel like there was something more than this, something beyond this for both of us. Kind of like we could sit down and draw a new map for ourselves, find a place to go and explore together – see it all. Find our own place, you know? And, as last drinks were called that night, I told your father that I was going to go and sleep in my car. He stood up and linked his arm in mine. He walked me out the door to my car in the car park around the back, and just kind of stayed with me. We were kind of just together then, I suppose, love. It was like this heat between us. It was like this warm blanket. I dunno. It was like we found our place with each other and could do anything together, anywhere.

AND AS THE MONTHS PASSED, we kept telling ourselves we were going to go and find our place, keep looking till we found it.

After we'd been together about a year, he moved out here with me. And we kept telling ourselves that we were not of this land, like we were more than it or something; that together we could cross over all the boundaries and lines, over languages and time zones. That's how I'd describe our love in the beginning, Cyn: like a dream that belonged somewhere else. And I remember that we would spend our nights talking in bed and looking out the window, watching the bright constellations of stars above us twinkling like they knew we were about to go. The land so still around us and always silent, like it was ignoring us or something. Does that make sense? Shit. Probably not. I don't bloody know. But that's how your father and I met. That's how it all started for us.

AND IN THOSE FIRST COUPLE OF YEARS out here together, your father bought the best Hereford bulls he could find to service the females, sowed plants for the herd as the land around us gave them so much. He fixed my father's tractor and put new roofs on the cattle sheds, was out there from dawn to dusk trying to make it work. Fatten the beasts up. Get them to market weight. A vet visit once every six months to vaccinate them and make sure everything was okay. He was certain that the wet would stay. And after you were born, love, just a few years later, the drought hit and your father would come home exhausted and overcome with it all, each month telling me that it was the driest on record, that he wasn't sure we would make it out here, that he knew my inheritance money was running out. And it was.

We sat down with a few coldies one night and talked about what to do. Should we sell the herd to another farmer? (*Who'll bloody buy it, love?*) Should we try to see if the abattoir would buy them at the weight they were? (*Who'll bloody buy young underweight cattle?*) I asked him if it was time for us to walk away, for the three of us to pack up and go, like we had dreamt of doing. Leave it all behind and go to Germany, Rome, Portugal, Spain. I stood up and took the tablecloth off the table and held it with two hands in front of him, swayed it back forth as if I was a matador. *We don't belong here, love*, I said to him. But he put his head in his hands, ignored me, his thoughts caught up in a landscape that was consuming him, kind of like it was eating him away. And I remember that we sat at the kitchen table for the longest time that night, looking out the window and into the darkness around us. We sat in silence, unsure of what we were a part of. We sat there for the longest time, Cyn. You could hear a bloody pin drop. And your father finally looked over at me and said that he would get a job at the abattoir to help us get through this rough patch, that they were still driving in cattle from other places around the state, the big cattle operations with feedlots. *No need for grassland or dams when you got 'em all stuck in a pen on top of each other. They fatten up quick too, just squashed up against each other all day without moving.* And I nodded at him and didn't say a word, knew how strange it was that while our cattle starved out on the land, only forty-five minutes away overfed Herefords were standing in a loading pen waiting to be slaughtered by the dozen. That night, Cyn, I knew that things had changed for us; that your father had been captured by this place.

YOUR FATHER STARTED WORKING at the abattoir the next month. He worked the night shift and then came home early in the morning smelling of the lemony gel they used in the showers there. He had a coffee and a bowl of beef stew (his favourite; I wonder if it still is?), then he'd get dressed in his overalls and his boots, give you a quick kiss and go and stand on the front verandah. He'd roll two smokes and smoke them one after the other. Yell out a goodbye to us and then walk down the stairs, jump in the ute and head out to tend to the cattle. You know, love, it's like he just slowly ran out of steam for me – for us, really. Like a wind-up toy or something. Like his mind was overtaken by trying to keep the property going through the day and paying our bills as he worked the floor at the abattoir at night. I guess with all that rolling around in his head, there wasn't much room for dreaming about new places with me.

—

AND YOU WERE A GOOD KID, CYN, an easy home birth. Shit, we didn't even get a nurse out here to help. Your father was a pro, though; he'd birthed a few calves in his time, you know. *Hands of a doctor*, I remember saying to him after you were born and we both sat on the lounge room floor, taking it in turns to hold you. Bloody lucky this place has got wooden floors is all I can say, love. Those were still good times when you were young. Even though I knew things had changed, we were still okay. Your father came back to life a bit after you came along. He stayed home a bit more, got the neighbour's young kid to come and do some work around the place to lessen the load here. I remember there was one night when he'd had a few beers and he started to talk about how the three of us could travel together. He really wanted to take us to the Whitsundays, had seen an ad for it in the local paper. Gosh, Cyn. It was only one night, but I remember it so well. I was so full of bloody hope.

And you would sleep all the time, waking when your father got up to go to the abattoir, then going back to sleep until I got up. Bloody good kid. Back then, your father and I still cuddled at night, and I asked him questions and he kind of answered. It was sort of like when we'd first met. But over time it was like he was this big, tight, full balloon that just kept losing air and getting smaller and weaker each year. Yeah, that's what he was like. His skin will be all shrivelled when he gets older, just like a saggy old balloon. But then I got pregnant with Mallory.

EVER SINCE THE DAY YOUR SISTER WAS BORN, I've been afraid of how this would end. You were ten, remember? Your father was spending all his time out on the land by then. Was never home anymore. Sometimes he'd take the ute and head off for the night. No idea where he went; he didn't speak much about it. There was only the three of us, wasn't there, when you weren't at school? And Mallory's constant noise. It was all her noise, all the bloody time. It's like that noise of hers had a life of its own after it left her mouth. Like it was crawling over the chairs and sitting on top of us. Like she was trying to drown us in her sound. I had no idea how to stop her. No idea. I tried, Cyn. I really tried. She wasn't like you.

DO YOU REMEMBER HOW I asked your father to take us to the doctor to get her looked at, but he said that it was because I wasn't feeding her enough or giving her enough cuddles? My fault. And yeah, looking back, I suppose it was. I was always so tired when I was with her. She kind of made me sad. Yeah, sad. And to be honest, all I really wanted to do that year was leave you both here and take off. Leave your father too, I guess. I didn't care where I went. I just knew there was more than this bloody place, this bloody life, this bloody feet-in-the-quicksand. That's the only way I can describe it to you, Cyn: it was like I was stuck.

And there was the afternoon I moved all my clothes and the lamp into the back room. Do you remember holding on to my leg and screaming at me that I didn't love your Daddy anymore? Do you remember Mallory lying in her basinet in your room screaming, screaming, screaming – fuck she never stopped unless you held her, did she? Remember me telling you over and over again that Mummy needed to be on her own sometimes, that there were things you would understand one day? Or maybe not. I still can't understand my sadness or your father's silence, or the pressure on my skull whenever Mallory opened her mouth. That day you stood in front of me with your hands on your hips and told me that I couldn't move in to that room? I tried to grab you and cuddle you, but you backed up against the wall and crossed your arms hard against your chest. My heart was such a mess that day, Cyn, and I didn't know how to tell you that I might hurt Mallory, really hurt her, if I didn't lock myself away.

I remember the next morning, as I heard Malloy screaming, the sun all over the room made it look like it was on fire. My body kinda ached all over. I'd never felt like that before, love. That day and night. Eight p.m. Nine p.m. Nine thirty. A bit past twelve. Each hour a different sound from her. It was like she was in the walls, in the floorboards, at the base of my skull, in my ears. Bloody everywhere. Until four a.m. Nothing. She was silent, and I sat on the bed waiting for the next sound. Nothing. I pulled my knees up to my chest and I heard you with her, heard you beside her. Your ear was to her mouth, I think. *Shhhh, shhhh now*, I heard you say. I sat there imagining her cheeks going that pink-red colour and, Cyn, I cried. I cried a lot. And it was tight or ripping or something, like there was some big war happening underneath the skin. I felt like my body was coming undone.

MALLORY'S FIRST BIRTHDAY PARTY. Do you remember the weeks leading up to it? I'd spent hours crafting: pasting and gluing and folding, making invites for her party. Blue cardboard with glitter all around the edges. Pictures cut out from old magazines that my mother had kept in a small cupboard under the house. I had finished the invites a month before her birthday, and one evening I asked your father to post them when he went into town the next day. Once a week he went. Do you remember? Always returning to us with fresh vegetables, meat from the abattoir – cheap deals for employees. A carton of beer, sometimes two. We did both like a drink back then. He sat at the dining room table looking at the cuts in his hands. You know, Cyn, back then is when his lips started to stick together. Like he had mud in his mouth. Like it had set hard or something. And his dry sweat smelt like the sun mixed with grass and cattle shit. I have no idea why; it's not like there was much grass left around here. It was like his body had started to fade into the land. It was a strange thing to witness. And all that romance and wanting to move and explore the world was never mentioned. I remember that night, you looked up at us and said, *Yes, yes, Mummy, Daddy hears you all the time* as your father sat there still staring at his hands. But he smiled like he always did whenever you spoke. He always smiled for you.

**REMEMBER THE DAY OF YOUR SISTER'S PARTY?** The two of you sat at the lounge room window watching for Rebecca and Melissa from a few properties down, for your father to come around the bend. Do you remember the streamers I made out of green cardboard, the fairy bread on that silver plate my mother had left, those big jugs of lemonade, your sister in a little jumpsuit with glittery blue arms to match the invites? I'll never forget your outfit that morning, Cyn. I laughed so hard when you walked out into the lounge room dressed all in black. An old black dress of mine, black stockings that must have once belonged to my mother, a purple bow in your hair. You'd even used eyeliner to make your lips black. *You told me that I could choose, Mum.* And my face was up against yours, our noses touching, as I told you that you could wear the dress all day long. You slept in it that night and the next. A week later you were still wearing it every day after school, and smelling like all the other bloody goths in Queensland, I suspect.

The three of us sat together in the lounge room waiting for the party guests. One p.m. Two. Your sister's ranting and yelling and talking were the only sounds. And when night-time came, your father walked in the front door and saw a table full of cakes and sweets and sodas, saw us still sitting on the couch, all upset. He walked past us mumbling that he forgot to send the invites, that it wasn't the end of the world, that Mallory would never remember it anyway. Do you remember your sister's loud screaming, her little glittered arms grabbing at me? Do you remember that I pushed her off? Your arms were strong enough to hold her then. *Take her to your room, take her.* You stood up and walked with her back to your room, humming the tune of her favourite nursery rhyme in her ear.

That night, after I turned the lights out, your father knocked on my door and told me he was sorry, that he didn't know how to tell me the things he wanted to. He lay down in the hallway with his ear to the gap under the door as I fell asleep. And that night I dreamt I was in Cambodia, Cyn – my feet bare in the back of a tuk-tuk, my hands holding on to the roof as the driver took a sharp corner. I heard women all around me speaking in foreign tongues. The next morning, I opened my door to tell your father about the dream, but he wasn't there; he had taken the ute and left. He was gone for a week. He never told me where he went.

FOR MONTHS AFTER Mallory's first birthday party, your father and I didn't speak a word to each other, and he came and went as he pleased. Sometimes he left in the ute, other times on the tractor or his bike. I never asked where he went. Looking back now, I suppose I had just stopped caring. And on the nights that he didn't come home, I'd grab a knife and take it with me to bed. I was afraid, or suspicious, of the noise Mallory made. Like, it wasn't natural, love. It had this weird otherworldly feel to it. I dunno how to explain it. But I wasn't taking any chances – a woman out here in the middle of nowhere with two kids, one of 'em a bit not right, isn't something you wanna be a part of. Trust me.

Do you remember the night when you ran to my door and bashed on it so hard to tell me that Mallory had taken her first step? I didn't say a word back to you, and you kicked my bloody door so hard that the house shook. But, darling, know that I heard you, that I stood on the other side of this door and cried. Cyn, know that I will always wonder how her little legs unfolded as she started to stand, if they lifted high, if they moved quickly. I will always wonder if she walked into your outstretched arms. I sat crying that night when you asked me if I was coming out to see. You stood there waiting for me to answer you, and I remember being so still and wishing I was in Cambodia, like I had dreamt, or any other place, really. All around me that night, the maps of all those unvisited counties and places. I could sense your anger, Cyn. A mother knows, can feel, can tell these things. I knew you were angry at me. That you still are. Do you remember telling me when Mallory had said her first full sentence? I do. But what I remember most was the sound of your voice when you told me. You weren't a kid anymore, Cyn. You were a young woman. I thought back to when you had first started talking. Your first word was broom. Did you know that? You'd run around the house saying, *Broom, broom, broom.* Your father used to grab the broom out of the laundry and get you to pretend to fly on it like a witch. It was the cutest bloody thing seeing you do that. Did you know that on your fifth birthday he bought you a witch's outfit from the op shop in town? Pointed hat. A black cape. Your father and I dressed up as wizards and I made us fondue, told you that the pot of bubbling cheese was a cauldron, that the carrots were the fingers of young girls who stole bread, that the pecans were the brains of women who asked too many questions. There are pictures around here somewhere of that night. You ate it all, and the table was covered in cheese/brain juice at the end of the night. Remember how you wouldn't drink the red cordial when I told you that it was the blood of the witch's victims? We laughed so hard.

That night at my door, you placed your mouth over the keyhole and yelled at me that you'd been teaching Mallory for months, that you had written a whole page full of her sentences. Did I want to see it? *Yes, yes, yes.* But I couldn't say it out aloud. And you slid it under my door anyway, remember? Your writing neat and in the brightest red ink. You stood still on the other side of the door as I held her words in front of me. I heard you breathing and imagined you were smiling in the way those women used to smile in that pub where I met your father. A triumphant kind of smile, I suppose. I read each line, each letter that you wrote. *She hates me. She keeps away from me. The bruises. From her. The red marks. From her. She hates me. I make my bed every day. She never sees it. She is locked in there and won't come out. She hates me.*

DO YOU REMEMBER ME TEACHING YOU how to make toasted sand-wiches back then? All the different kinds of ingredients you could use. Cheese and tomato. Banana – always butter and sugar on the outside to make it crispy. Mince and onion, or marshmallows and strawberries. You wrote shopping lists, mastered how to clean the toilet without splashing bleach all over the tiles. Do you remember how I placed a small box under your pillow one day when you were out roaming the land with Mallory, looking for the 'hidden treasure' your father had told her about in his attempt to get you and your sister away from me? (I would see him walking around outside sometimes in the early mornings with handfuls of lollies or small stones wrapped in aluminium foil, bending down to hide them.) Do you remember that box of pads and tampons with a brochure from Tampax showing you how to use them? We never spoke about it, did we? I'd had it ready for you for years. I remember the words *Petal Soft* on the front of that blue-and-pink tampon packet – made me laugh out loud, love. Who'd want a bloody petal shoved up them? I remember thinking. How would a petal hold all your blood? Ha! Ad men, eh? Forever confused and scared of our bodies. Oh, and don't forget the ads on the telly for panty liners – the ones 'wrapped individually for your convenience' – that we used to laugh at together. You were around twelve when I found a small drop of blood on the toilet seat, and I knew you wouldn't come and ask me what was going on. I thought it best to let you work it out for yourself. Leaving that box under your pillow is the last thing I remember doing for you back then.

—

AND THAT YEAR THE HEADACHES CAME. They were like a pounding in my skull that made me lose balance and get confused. I'd left a note on the kitchen table asking your father to get me a few boxes of Mersyndol from the chemist in town, and I found myself sleeping all day and coming out at night to wander the house when no one was around. Those pills were so bloody nice. Like soft clouds around my skull. I remember how well you looked after Mallory, after the house – made sandwiches, roast chicken, chocolate slices. I was always so tired, always curled up in a ball on this bed. I put in my earplugs and buried my head in the pillow to muffle the sound of her crying. Her voice running all over my skin and pushing down into my ears, my eyes, my mouth; hitting at my gums and the spaces between my teeth. I didn't shower for weeks on end, didn't leave my room. Your father sometimes stopped at my door when he came home early in the morning. He'd whisper that he would love me forever and he promised me a trip one day, when you had both grown up, when the land gave a little back, when he'd saved more money, when I felt better, when the fences were fixed. When. When. When. But he didn't mean it. He'd only speak to me with a door between us. Looking back now, I reckon he just did that to make himself feel okay about what he was doing when he left us here in the house. You know, Cyn, I asked him on one of these nights when he was sitting at the door where he went when he took the ute. I remember he sat silent for ages and eventually said, *I don't know what this all is anymore, love.* That's it, Cyn, that's all he said. That's all he could give me.

THAT YEAR, I'd lie in bed remembering my childhood in the city. (Climbing out my bedroom window to go down to the local skate park. Richard's dinner of steak and mash – *Make sure it's steaming bloody hot, girl* – made and served by four p.m. Me begging him to let me go to school – *Please, please, I promise I won't cause any problems.* Shaving my legs for the first time with his rusted razor. Trying my first sip of beer from a can that I'd stolen out of the fridge. My hair so long that I learnt how to plait it. The boy next door who used to write poems to me then throw them through the window wrapped around stones.) In bed that year out here, I started imagining the new places I could go to, Cyn. I'd have the weirdest dreams too. Shit, the dreams were so vivid that sometimes I wasn't even sure if I was asleep or awake. There'd be all these women talking to me. All different accents and different ages. But it felt really real, like it wasn't a dream at all, and it was like they all knew me or something. But I'd never see them, just hear them. I dreamt of sitting on a beach in Bali. I dreamt of being with a group of young women, driving together in an old van across America's Route 66. Of walking, of bending down and picking up rocks on a road that never ended.

Of maps, of places, of moving from here. The dreaming, Cyn, their voices, it just didn't stop.

Do you remember coming to my door each morning and asking if I would come out? You'd ask me about things I hadn't taught you yet. How much powder to put in the washing machine. How to Mallory-proof the low kitchen cupboards. How many bowls of jelly you should let her eat. Did I ever answer you? I don't think I did, did I? I'd sit on my bed all day, and in the afternoon watch this room become fire as the sun turned in for the night. I'd hear you talk and laugh with Mallory as you cooked just outside my door, heard you clean up and place your father's meal on the table, hoping he would come home. After you both went to bed, I'd open my door and walk out into the dark house. I'd stand and look at the dining room table where we used to sit together each night. I'd imagine us all together, laughing and talking about our days. I'd mouth conversations with empty chairs, lean down to kiss the air near your father's imagined head while he looked up at me with a big smile. I'd walk over to the lounge room windows and look out at the land around us, then I'd go to the kitchen, get a knife, walk back to my room and place it under my pillow, ready. Cyn, I used to stab the air with those knives, stabbed Mallory's voice as I lay there in the dark, stabbed those women when I woke. Stabbed. Stabbed, but they just never stopped.

—

I FIRST HEARD THEM when I was awake the year Mallory turned three. They were a really soft sound at first, and I thought it was you and Mallory whispering about me. You were always huddled together whispering something in your bedroom with those bloody encyclopedias in front of you. I'd lie in bed and listen to you whispering for hours, sometimes kicking at the walls to make you stop when I couldn't take it anymore. When you kept on whispering I thought that you were just being smartarses. But as the voices grew louder and louder I realised that they weren't you at all – it was women I'd never met, women I'd once known from town. One night, I even heard your grandmother. Your father had been gone for three days, and I was roaming the house after you and Mallory went to bed. As I walked into the kitchen, I heard my mother's voice. It sounded like she was gargling water; her words were fading in and out. I stood still and looked all around me. My knife was up and at the ready. I heard my mother say Mallory's name, my name. I heard her say the name of her own mother, *Joan*, her mother's mother, *Norma*, and go on to recite a list of names that I assume were the women in our family that came before us. Then she faded out again. Her voice disappeared as the sound of water overtook her one last gasp. After that night, I started to bandage the top of my head with cling wrap before I slept. I crept around the house at night, and all these women – they were mashing up against my skull. I tried dipping balls of cotton wool in turps and putting them in my ears to stop them. Who bloody knows why I thought cling wrap and turps would work? They didn't, of course; the voices just kept coming.

One night, as I walked around the house, I looked in on you both cuddled up together in your bed, exhausted. I'd heard you all afternoon trying to settle your sister, to stop her tantrums, her screaming. Giving her time out in the bathroom. Her throwing soap and shampoo bottles up against the locked door. Your breath breaking into near sobs as you stood in the kitchen making curried sausages and rice for dinner. You promising her things I knew you could never give her (a fairy party, a new Barbie doll, a raspberry slushie – *the biggest paper cup they have*), anything to make her stop. A mother's tone in your voice. Me. Love, you sounded just like me. I stood watching you both sleep as your sister's voice rose above all the other voices. She was saying my name over and over, telling me that nobody had ever loved me, or her. That we/her/you didn't belong here. She kept saying my name, love. And I leant over to put my hand over her mouth, to quiet her, but her body was still and her eyes were shut; her mouth open and snoring. Your hand was resting on her chest as it lifted up and down with her breath. And right then, Cyn,

I thought that I was mad, crazy, batshit loco. I didn't know what to do except keep shutting myself in this back room away from you both.

AND IT WAS EVERY NIGHT. Mallory would scream and yell. Mallory would be asleep beside you. She was bloody everywhere. She'd tell me all the shitty things I'd done: not responding to her when she came to my door; pushing past her in the hallway; grabbing her around the head when she just wouldn't shut up; forgetting her favourite foods. She'd say that you both hated me, that I had driven your father away. She told me you had promised to take her away from me. Did you really do that? Did you?

And then one night your sister started describing the colour of her hair in the sun (Copper. Gold. Rusted). It was like fire, she said. Like the start of a huge fire. Her laugh was so wild and loud when she said this, and it swept in under my door like a cyclone. Imagine that, eh? It hit my cheeks as a storm surge, rolling around my gums and making my mouth move up and down with her vibrations. And there was the taste of blood. I spat it over the walls. Spat it everywhere. And your father was home that night, tinkering with the motorbike outside. But he didn't hear it. He didn't hear the women's voices, didn't hear

Mallory. Didn't notice a thing. He'd stopped talking to us by then, remember?

AFTER YOUR FATHER'S SILENCE SET IN, I'd listen to you and your sister trying so hard to make him talk. Your jokes. Standing on your head. Dressing your sister up in the clothes I'd left in his cupboard. Tickles on the couch. Putting a glass of water by his bed as he slept and putting his index finger in it to see if he would pee. Did he ever? I think that's an old wives' tale, love. I had been trying for years to get something out of him, but it was like that balloon of his was limp and tied to one of the front gate posts – just hanging there and getting dried out in the sun. I tried to make sense of his grunted-one-word responses. Pushed for answers that had no end and no beginnings. He had no bloody fearlessness or wonder left. All bloody gone, thanks to those long hours on the land and in the abattoir. He was exhausted, forgot that there was more than this for us. I wanted him to talk to me again, start daydreaming with me, leave this place with me. I wanted him to notice me. See what was going on. But he wouldn't, couldn't, anymore. He just didn't. And I thought about other ways to make him notice. I dressed up nicely and left my door ajar when I heard him in the house. He didn't come in. I left cards under his pillow with maps of all the places we could go together and notes detailing what we could do once we got there. I drew a map of New York City all in pink; its streets in that perfect grid system they have. Drew all the landmarks I remembered from magazines, described how we'd rent an apartment and go out for coffee all the time, take a carriage ride through Central Park. I drew another map in all different shades of purple, one in yellow, even one in grey – your father's favourite colour. I put so much work into that one for him, love. I even drew the pub where your father and I met, and the streets surrounding it. Drew the big brown Brisbane River winding its way in front of it, and the exact spot in the public bar that he asked me to play pool. He'd told me back then that I was *the most beautiful woman* he'd ever seen, standing under the lights in that bar, my hair *like a collection of fires burning out of control in a heatwave.* All the maps, all the countries and lands in the world led back to him, Cyn. I tried to make him understand that. But he just threw them away. I'd see them when I came out at night – the cards – crumpled up in the kitchen bin.

REMEMBER WHEN I ASKED YOU to post that letter on your way to school and told you not to read it? Did you anyway? I'd written a personal ad for the paper. And men started to call me as soon as that ad went in. Like the same bloody night. *Hey there, keen for a chat? Maybe you're the kind of girl that likes a bit of an older bloke?* And there were so many calls. *Do you like a man with a bit of stubble on his face? How about you tell me how big I feel inside of you?* I'd stand in the hallway in the dark as they told me things about themselves – *married, divorced, living in the caravan park in town.* They told me other things that I wouldn't want to repeat to you, to be honest, love. Your father was so rarely home by then. Or maybe he was sometimes. I don't know. One fella who called suggested he come over to visit, that he would make it worth my while. *Bit of extra cash for you to buy yourself something pretty.* I was willing to try anything by that stage to get your father to touch me, hold me – to get him so bloody angry when he heard me on the phone that he'd come out and scream at me, push me, slap me on the face so I could feel the sting of his skin on mine. Our bodies remembering: the want, the pleasure, the refuge in each other – that longed-for other life.

I REMEMBER THE FIRST TIME ONE OF THEM CAME OVER – it was Peter from the drive-through bottle shop in town. You kids were in bed already, and I stood in the dark at the kitchen window and watched as his headlights reached the house. Saw his shadow step out of the car. Heard his heavy steps come up the front stairs, opened the door and smiled at him, told him to take his thongs off so he wouldn't wake you girls when he walked up the hallway. I remember he handed me a cold tallie of XXXX for us to drink together as we sat down on the bed, said it would *calm our nerves*, that he'd *never done anything like this before.* We sat side by side drinking, our thighs touching, and he reached into his pocket and took out a pile of twenty-dollar notes – *buy something pretty for yourself.* He undid the buttons on his shirt as I opened the top drawer of the bedside table and put the cash he'd given me into a little sequined purse – the one your father won for me at the chocolate wheel in Sideshow Alley at the Brisbane Ekka when we first started going out. He took off all his clothes and told me to take off my pants and my underwear and, well, Peter and I fucked that night, Cyn, shook the old fibro walls. He made me climb on top of him and – *Ride me, ride me like a fucking bull.* His sour boozy scent the only thing I could smell wafting up. One, two, three . . . Shit, I dunno, it didn't take long for him to come.

I remember each one, Cyn. Their sounds, the pattern of their breath. John – Rebecca and Melissa's dad from a few properties down – would come to sit on the edge of the bed and tell me about how unhappy he was while I massaged his feet. He just couldn't deal with a whole house full of women, he'd say. You remember those girls, don't you, Cyn? And there was Rob from the abattoir who would fuck me loudly; the idea that your father might catch us a turn-on for him. I imagined all those women who floated around me talking all the time were stunned into silence. They never made a peep when the men were here. It was a relief. There were some strange men in this room with me that year . . . An old bloke called George; something wrong with that one. There was your first-grade teacher, Mr Pearson, and his son – Scotty, I think his name was. How bloody odd to fuck someone with your boy. Weird, Cyn. Just weird. There was a handful of your father's younger workmates (Richard, Trev and a bloke who I only remember because of his hair – same colour as ours, love. Skinny bugger he was). There was Dave, chief of the local fire brigade, and a bloke who spoke too much; I never did catch his name. I wonder why, eh? Don't think your father didn't know – he did. But I guess he just didn't know what to do anymore. Thought that I just didn't love him. Gosh, love, a part of me wanted him to get so bloody angry, to take me away from them all, take me away from this whole place. He didn't. And after each of the men left, I'd go downstairs and wash my bedsheets, stand out in the moonlight and hang them up. I'd look up at your father's bedroom window and wonder if he was home. Once, only once, did I see his shadow behind the lace curtains just standing and looking back at me. He had heard bloody everything, Cyn.

But mostly I was alone, and those women's voices made a racket around me. They fought, they bickered. Some voices said I was a whore, others said it was my body and I could do what I bloody well wanted with it. Some said I was misunderstood. Others just made noises in their throat or coughed. One night, I lay here on the bed stabbing at them with my knives, yelling at them that I was confused. Confused about who they were and where they came from, why they kept coming back. I yelled at them that I didn't know what was happening to me, didn't understand what this life had become for the four of us. And I put on my dressing-gown and walked into the lounge room to get away from them. But their voices followed me and kind of took up residence, moved in to all the corners they could fit – into the moulding on the ceiling, the slits in the floorboards, under the cushions on the couch, on top of the television and in the folds of the curtains. *Come, come, follow us*, said a voice. I realised it was your sister, and I stood still, holding a knife in front of me, scared of her, scared of what I would do to her. *Come, follow us, Mum.* Her voice was bloody unmistakable in the dark, Cyn. Her laugh. She ran up the hallway and circled me. That wild laughter. Her sounds tightening like a rubber band around my head. (How much can a rubber band stretch until it breaks? How much can a heart take until it breaks?) I held the knife tight. *Come see, Mum.* But Cyn, I had no idea what she meant, where she wanted me to go. I walked up the hallway and into your bedroom. You were both asleep. Her eyes, her mouth closed. Her arms pushed up to her chest and you holding her, like you always did. I moved closer to you both. I leant down to touch her face, and her laughter was so loud. I remember that you woke up to see me standing above you, and you jumped up and grabbed at the knife in my hand, so I began slapping her to wake her up, to try to stop the sound. It didn't work. You were both so freaked out, remember? You screamed and pushed me away. You said, *What the fuck are you doing?* Do you remember saying that? And you pushed me again. You pushed me out of the room.

It was Mallory, Mallory, Mallory's voice in my head. And that night, I grabbed the box of Mersyndol, a bottle of your father's whisky, his keys and walked down the front steps. Got in the ute. Started it. *Join us.* I heard those women's voices, Cyn, louder than I ever had before. They were cheering me on like fans at a football game. They were. Whoop. Whoop. Whooping. They were a whole grandstand of fans. They were Friday night drinks to blow off steam. And all those voices. A woman named Petra told me that she'd had her head pushed under the water when she wouldn't fuck her date. Carol, with a thick Irish accent, told me she was made to sit at the back of the room by her teacher. It was like a wall of bloody sound. Like a gathering or something – all the voices crossing over each other and all complicated. And I drove, Cyn. Trying to get away from them. Their sound. Their voices. Their stories. Fast. Faster. Every turn of the wheel, every telephone pole, every kilometre, hoping that it would stop. A few Mersyndol. A swig of whisky to wash them down. I don't even remember driving into town or parking in front of the abattoir. Who knows why I did that? I was probably thinking your father'd have to take notice of me there when he turned up for his morning shift. Shit, I dunno. But the last thing I remember that night was the feeling of soft clouds around my skull from the drugs, and the taste of sweet woody chemicals from the whisky. I'm sure I was being held in the arms of a fat woman who was softly singing, *Hey, cunt, cunt. Hey, you're a fat, fat, fat cunt, fat, fat cunt.* My eyes heavy-closing. *My name is Mary, love. I was killed by a group of men who were angry that I was taking up too much space on a bus seat.* (All the women taking up all those spaces in a world not made for them I suppose, eh, Cyn?) My head dropping, the feeling of drool running down my cheek, and waking the next morning to the sound of tapping. Tap. Tap. Your father leaning down in his work whites and looking at me through the window. (*There he is on the street with his crazy whore wife – fuck knows why he's still with her.*) And, I knew that I was the crazy woman, an insane wife, as your father said to me, *Love, put your bloody top back on. Put it on now. Why the hell are you parked out here?* I looked down at my breasts and the empty bottle of whisky sitting between my legs. He stood back with his hands on his hips. *I had to hitch a ride to work this morning 'cause the tyre's flat on the bike and you took the bloody ute, didn't you. For fuck's sake.*

That morning, your father didn't walk in the gates to the abattoir. Instead, he drove me home in silence. He looked at me as we pulled up to the house and said, *Get your bloody shit together, love. Your daughters deserve better than this.* I moved slowly up the stairs and ignored you both as you came running down the hallway towards me. I pushed your sister away as she grabbed at my leg. She fell down and hurt her ankle, remember? That night, your father stayed home and I went into his room and sat on the edge of the bed, woke him with a small push on his shoulder. I told him everything: about the voices, about Mallory being both here and there – wherever *there* was. About the rubber band tightening around my head. And he sat up and held me. He held me. That night, he lay beside me and held me without saying a word.

THAT WEEK YOUR FATHER called in all manner of people to *rid me of my madness* – the local priest, some tarot card reader he met at the pub (*fucking hippie*), even the old birds from the op shop in town. The acts of a desperate man, Cyn. He had no bloody idea. And I stayed in my room, didn't even come out at night anymore. I sat biting my fingernails down to the quick, the voices rolling and pushing and just keeping on at me. *Yolanda. Sylvia. Dorothy* as one looping bloody sound. Whoop. Whoop. Whoop. Circling around each other. Like a thousand pots and pans being banged at the same time. Like a group of cars in a collision. Like nails being hammered into a sheet of metal. Like the sound of those afternoon storms that break the heat – the ones that we always wished for together, remember? They told me the names of their daughters, of their friends, their unborn daughters, their sisters. They told me the ways in which they were taken, hurt, lost. All of it. And I sat on my bed moving my head back and forth, trying to rid myself of their whispers, their thumps, their stories, their screaming bloody fucking murder in my ears. I stayed in my room, Cyn. I couldn't let you see me like this. I could never let you know what I'd become. I lost my appetite then, too, do you remember? The food that you left by my door before you went to bed was hardly touched, except by the ants. I was living on those salty crackers and bottles of Coke your father bought in bulk last year. The salt and acid in my stomach reminding me that I was still real. I lost weight. My collarbones stuck out straight like rulers.

COME, MUM, COME WITH ME. Your sister's voice is the loudest. *Come, Mum.* She says it over and over again. Sometimes her voice is joined by that of another young girl who has an English accent. *Come*, they say, *come, come.* She is here, she is there, she is nowhere or wherever that was or wherever that is or wherever it could be. At the same time she is out there with you – all flesh and blood and breathing. It's like she's this weird link between life and death. She is all sound. She runs and catches fairies outside my window. She is in the bed with you. She is deep in my ears and under my covers and holding hands with a dead woman I've never met before. She is climbing trees and crouching under rocks out on the land. She is in this house and out there with all of them. She is seen but not seen, and she is my madness come to life. And Cyn, I don't know what to do.

MALLORY IS CRYING AT MY DOOR. Stop her, Cyn. I hear her. She's crying. You're hushing her. I can hear your voice close to her face. You're telling her not to be too loud, that today is my birthday. Today is my birthday. I hear her ask if she can make me cupcakes, the ones with hundreds and thousands on top in all the colours of the rainbow. Ask if that will make me happy again. You don't answer her. You both go quiet.

I hear her out there with you, punching the walls. I hear her in my mouth. I hear her breath under the voices of all these women, Cyn. I am standing at the door now. She's yelling and banging on it. She's pushing against it. She's been walking in circles around the kitchen for the last five minutes. My ear is pressed up against the keyhole. My hands are around my ankles as I sit and listen, and rainclouds are pushing in under the door. She's knocking now, she's screaming at me. You are holding her, hushing her, grabbing at her like a mother should. Stop her. Stop her from coming near me, Cyn. Fuck. There's a pounding at the window. The door. I hear Mallory outside the door. I hear her at the window with the little English girl, with my own mother, with all of them. She is inside, she is outside. She is about to break glass all over me. She is about to push through my skull (rubber-band-breaking – this is how long it takes). And they are all here – those women – hundreds of them. They're moving over me and chanting their names and their stories, Cyn. The throbbing in my head. They are forming a circle around me, and one is holding Mallory in her arms. Cyn, I'm so sorry. Know that I'm sorry. She's starting a fire at my temples. She's got her whole body up against the door. I'm going. I'm going. I'm, going to open the bedroom door now.

# THE FRAYED END

BACK THEN, JUST BEFORE IT HAPPENED, I'd walk in slow circles around the house listening for her in that back room. We hadn't heard from our mother for days and our father had been gone for weeks. Mallory and I had worked out months beforehand where he went to when he rode his motorbike up to the top paddock. We'd followed him one morning (hiding behind an old tractor, a cow, a fallen tree so that he didn't see us) as he rode out towards the foot of the hills. We saw him stop at the old unused shed, get off his bike and pat one of the Herefords that were grouping under the old river red gums, the creamy bark and white flowers hanging low to the ground. When he went inside, we ran quietly up to the window, and I stood up on a rusted wheel rim to look in, saw him sitting on a pile of hay that was covered in blankets, his elbow up in the air as he smoked, staring up at the ceiling. Around him, an old wooden bench covered in packets of milk arrowroot biscuits and long-life milk, a gas lamp attached to a bottle, a metal bucket with water in it on the floor. A towel. A face washer. Two pairs of dirty jeans hung over a broken chair. This, I realised as I stepped back down to Mallory, who was eager to know what he was doing in there, was the place he came – the place he came to get away from the three of us. This was his neutral territory, between us and his new life.

JUST BEFORE IT HAPPENED, he took the HQ and left us without a way to get anywhere, for. An emergency, for. Food from town, and. Sometimes, now, I remember it all, every little detail. Sometimes, it's like an unmade puzzle, an unfinished sentence, a knitted jumper that's unravelling. My memories fold in and around each other, roll out onto my hot open palm.

THAT MORNING BEFORE IT HAPPENED was a Saturday, was my mother's birthday, and Mallory had woken me. Jumping on me, pushing her nose into my belly button. *It's her birthday, it's her birthday. Will Mum be happy today?* My hands reached down to cover her mouth as she said this, and I told her that I didn't know, that it was best to wait and see. She was all spirit and force that morning. Jumping. Jumped morning-brightness. She was out of bed and running to our mother's room. She was bashing on her door and screaming, *Mum! Mum! Come out and say hello!* And, when she didn't respond, *Cake, cake! Mum . . . Mum, I want to cuddle you. Mum. Just open the door, Mum!* My sister was a thunder of words, her face crimson, her body an unruly mass of excitement. I ran up behind her and held her (grab her by those small arms, lift her, place your hands over her mouth, bend her body forward to crush her lungs – no good comes from girls or women who speak out of turn). Started kissing her all over her cheeks, and. Saw my father walking into the kitchen with his swag over his shoulder and a cardboard box full of vegetables – or maybe it was beer, maybe. Or maybe he had nothing – maybe. I do remember clearly, though, that he was wearing a button-up shirt I'd never seen him in before, and that he stood still with his eyes firmly on me, not saying a word. I looked over at him as (time moves slowly in the base of my skull remembering this moment, a heated and hollering slowness I can never forget) an aberration. (I remember learning at school that, in astronomy, an aberration is the displacement of a heavenly body, owing to the motion of the Earth in its orbit – what grand displacement this was before me.) All spirit and force, Mallory screamed at me to let her go. She wriggled out of my arms and started bashing on our mother's door, and. Our father walked over to the bench and put down the box, turned to us, and I'm sure he said, *Leave your mother alone, Mallory.* He rubbed his brow. *Cyn, love, I'm gonna go and sleep somewhere else tonight, best if I do.* Mallory ran to him, reached up for him. I think. I think she did. I think she hung off his legs as he crossed his arms, stood as stiff as a board, as vacant as some of the old shopfronts in town. And he should have told me then; should have told me that everything would be okay, that he'd take care of this. I stood glaring at him as he pushed Mallory away. *What the fuck are you going to do about this, Dad? What the fuck are you going to do about her in there?* And he turned away from us, his neck turning a bright-brilliant red. *Go back to your whore in the city. Go on,* I must have yelled at him – must have, and. I remember that his dry hands reached for the top of his head. His hands shook. He walked right back out of the house.

I picked Mallory up by the waist and carried her back to our bedroom. I threw her on the bed, slammed the door behind us, stood and watched as she sobbed herself into still silence. I sat in the chair under our bedroom window that morning and watched as her breathing slowed, as her eyelids fluttered with confusion. I watched as she turned her head and asked me for something to drink. I got up and went to the kitchen, poured her a glass of cordial – or milk, maybe – and took it to her. She sat up against the wall sipping her drink and asked me if our mother had come out yet. *No.* She put her drink on the floor beside the bed and asked me if we could make her a birthday cake. *We shouldn't.* She asked if we could make her a birthday card. *No.* I sat back down in the chair and read one of my father's old copies of *Reader's Digest* as the sun rose to its peak, read the last pages as it started slowly moving towards its guaranteed setting. Its golden reflections pushed off the land, bounced off our bedroom mirror and the glass jars that Mallory had put on the windowsill – filled with old bones and coloured food dye. Together they shone as a kaleidoscope of sorrow on the bedroom floor. And we sat together in the spectrum, in the band of colours that the sun passed through for us. We sat in violets, in. Apple greens, among. Zinc yellows, with. A mass of dark carmine orange streaming right onto Mallory's chest. We sat like this in silence for hours, Mallory finally speaking on dusk. Could we sing our mother a birthday song? We could make one up ourselves and perform it to her. *No, you know she doesn't like noise. We don't want to make her angry, especially on her birthday, do we?* Could we stay up late that night and surprise her as she walked down the hall? *No.* Could we climb with a ladder up the back of the house to look through her window? *No, we don't want her to be even more scared than she already is.* Could we make a large HAPPY BIRTHDAY banner out of an old bedsheet and hang it over her window? *No. No. No. It's time to make dinner.* And twelve steps to the fridge to get the beef mince out. Her small feet dancing so lightly on the amber-coated floorboards all around me, her wild hair spinning in the rising moonlight. Six steps. She stood still in the centre of the kitchen and started to mouth our mother's name, started to whisper it, say it, yell it – louder, yelling, louder, screaming our mother's name, and. Running around the house, and. Banging on the walls, and. Calling out her name like an incantation. Her body wild and uncontrollable, her mouth wide, and. In fiery concentration, she placed her humming lips over all the keyholes in the house, to the gaps in the floorboards, under our mother's door, inside cups, bowls, over my mouth. (Our mouths joined in our mother's name, and. I wonder would she have now sounded like me, would she have now sounded like our mother, would she have moved and taken a foreign accent?) My hands grabbing for her, me chasing her as she moved through the house like wildfire. Wild. Fire. And. The sound of movement from my mother's room. Wild. The door. Open. Her large against the gold-glittering light. I will never forget her standing there before us. (It had been weeks, months, it had been forever.) Her hair pulled back in a ponytail. Her old shirt stained. Her eyes dark grey. She told Mallory to come to her, come closer. (Hold on to her. Hold on to her for dear life. Hold on to everything that could ever matter.) We looked at our mother. (Move. Squirm. Get out of this grip. Go to her.) One step. Two. Five steps to her. The door closing, slamming, pushed softly. I don't know. My mother's hand on Mallory's back, urging her to the bed that was covered with paper and pens and sticky tape. I heard the door being locked from inside, and. I stood for the longest time and listened for them, heard whispering between them, heard my mother place a rolled-up towel at the base of the door to keep their sounds in, heard Mallory's muffled questions, a singalong, a booming laugh from my mother as the moon rose in the dark night sky.

THAT NIGHT, I JUMPED IN THE HQ (*move the gears in a seamless H, a seamless H*) and drove up to the to the top paddock looking for my father. With the lights on high beam, I stopped at the shed. Saw his motorbike out front, and. Walked in, saw the gas light on. Walked back out and called for him. *Dad? Dad, where the fuck are you? Something's happening at the house, Dad?* The pitch-black night absorbed everything around me, clouds covering the starlight that existed only in this moment to help me find him.

THAT NIGHT, I PACED AROUND THE KITCHEN. (It took nineteen steps to walk around the kitchen once; now it takes ten.) I paced until my legs started to ache. I walked down the front steps and out the back of the house, grabbed my father's ladder and climbed up, looked through her window full of dream catchers, saw reflections of silver under fluorescent light (knives, knives, her collection of knives – and all the things I could have done back then to stop this) and both of them huddled together on the bed. That night, there was only silence in the house, and. Standing in the kitchen alone, I guessed that they had fallen asleep, now curled up together, in the same position I had slept in with Mallory for years now. I put my ear to my mother's door and listened. Nothing. At the kitchen sink I poured a glass of water and drank it, and in our bedroom I got into my pyjamas and climbed into bed. I tossed. Turned. Tucked my feet in under the sheets. I held my breath to hear sounds. I looked up at the dark ceiling. Tried counting sheep, cattle, grass, one dry blade at a time.

I SLEPT HEAVILY, DREAMT IN COLOUR that night. Dreamt a mass of women's faces and bodies, dreamt in sounds that woke me screaming an hour before sunrise. As I got out of bed and turned on the bedroom light, I saw that my wrists were covered in breaking blood vessels which would, eventually, turn into bruises. A reminder, I thought, that dreaming was a physical thing, was a fury in my unconscious hours. I stood by my bedroom door and smelt smoke, I think (my father in the kitchen, burning toast or bacon – the smell of meat, fat falling off the bone?).

Looked for him through the keyhole. He wasn't there. No one was there, and. I heard my father. Heard him screaming, howling. I heard him wailing. I opened the bedroom door and raced to my mother's room – the door already open. There was no one inside. There was no one. No one. There was, the telephone receiver hanging by its cord in the hallway, smoke in my throat and on my lips, and the sound of my father's deep bellows all around me. The smell of smoke everywhere. At the wide-open front door there was a brightness, like daylight. There was the smell of fat, burning meat. There was my hand reaching for the verandah railing. There was time so slow. Slowing. There was a wall of heat hitting my face, and. There was my father, his screams deafening, held at the waist by a young cop and struggling to free himself – *You cunt, you crazy fucking cunt. Oh my little girl. My little girl.* His eyes were fixed on her little body still in the fire, and three young officers kicked away burning logs. Two of them jumped through flames to reach Mallory's small body. One of them stood by the edge of the fire with a hose in his hand. (This is my jumper with the thread that I've pulled now falling to the floor at my feet – this is where I'm not sure.) There was my mother, in the back of a cop car, not looking at anyone. Perhaps there was a warm blanket wrapped around my shoulders, the moving lips of regretful cops, the hissing sound of her skin melting into the dirt and all of us arriving too late to stop this from happening. *The call came from your wife, mate. We got here as soon as we could.* My father had got here as soon as he could too, I'm sure he said. On his motorbike from the shed when he saw the smoke, saw the flames. There was my father, the frayed end, the missed stitch, the loose piece of wool under the starless night sky. *Mate, we're so very sorry.*

# LITTLE BOY, LITTLE GIRL

DAYS LATER, I am walking in a circle around the lounge room, and the palms of my hands burn like fire. I have been crying. Underneath me are the glossy, the scratchy, the thickly, thinly, largely, the small. The ephemera found in my mother's hiding spot under the bed. I am gasping. Under my feet ink runs from the crumpled paper, bleeds onto the floorboards as a swirling bruise. (There is a madness that creeps in while you cry, don't you think – in between those gasps at air, those sobs, those silent spaces?), and.

—

I ONLY REMEMBER MY FATHER CRYING ONCE, sitting with my mother in the green-and-brown-striped lounge chair that's in front of me now. I was about three, I think, sitting in the corner with a handful of my mother's homemade playdough. Always bright blue – *so you can imagine swimming in the ocean, love.* I had never been to the beach back then. Still haven't, and. I remember my father sitting in the chair with my mother kneeling beside him, his head reaching up for the sky, his chest rising as he gasped in air, as he pulled back the tears so I wouldn't see. My mother rubbed her hand up and down the length of his arm, and he kept repeating the words, *El Niño, El Niño, fucking El Niño. We're never gonna make a go of it out here, love.* I had no idea what the words meant back then, but I remember running to him and jumping on him, saying them back to him, remember my mother pulling me off him and walking me to my bedroom. Her closing the door. Those few years were so dry out here, and we were only allowed to flush the toilet after we shit (*If it's yellow, let it mellow; if it's brown, flush it down*), only washed our clothes every second week (*We need to make sure the cattle get most of it, love*). Showers every third day, and the salty smell from my mother's armpits when she cuddled me. The rotten egg smell of bore water in everything we wore.

I never saw him cry again. But years later, when Mallory was about the same age I was back then, the local council filled the pool with water for the first time in a long while. I had never been in that much water before, and we were so excited as our father drove us there one day in summer, our legs sticking to the vinyl of the ute's bench seat. *Now, you promise you'll look after your sister? Yes, there are lifeguards, but if you ever want to come back here again, you better keep a bloody eye on her.* Our bodies that afternoon when he picked us back up, smelling of chlorine and aloe vera that he'd brought from the terracotta pot at the bottom of the front steps to soothe our sunburnt skin – the plant's brown tips a reminder that it too was fighting to survive out here. On the way home that afternoon, I was certain that I saw a tear roll down his cheek. Looking back now, it was all falling apart around that time. It was all falling apart for us. I guess.

YEARS AFTER I saw my father crying on the armchair in the lounge room, I summoned up the courage to ask him what El Niño meant. He stopped fixing the generator and looked up at me standing above him with my hands on my hips. *Gosh, Cyn, you've got a bloody memory on ya, don't ya? You're the smart one in the family, eh. Maybe you'll get to go to uni one day.* He patted the hard ground beside him and I sat down. *Well, think of it this way, love: when small changes happen in one part of the world, they can affect other parts of the world. Like turning your pedestal fan on in your room. You think it's only moving the air in front of you, but eventually the air it generates mixes with the whole room, the rest of the house, even out here to the rest of the property. You feel it the most because you're closest, but it also affects the outside here. It's the same for things that happen all around the world in the Earth's atmosphere — it's all air pressure and temperature. So El Niño is when water that's warmer than normal sits in the Pacific Ocean, and then comes over this way and changes the way things usually are. That's one of the reasons why we're so bloody dry out here.* I listened intently as I dug deep waves in the hard red dirt with a stick. *Did you know, Cyn, that El Niño — which is used to describe warm weather — means 'the little boy' in Spanish? And cold weather is called La Niña. It means 'the little girl'.* He turned from me and kept working on the generator as I sat beside him, digging the stick deeper into the earth, trying to make tidal waves. What he'd told me didn't mean much to me back then, but means a lot more to me now. Makes all kinds of sense. All kinds.

I AM STILL WALKING IN THE CIRCLE. Ten steps each turn and my mother's bruised world beneath me. One more step, and I hear them. I stop. I am fleshy and heavy-weighted in the sorrow that has moved from my mother to me, from her mother to her, from her mother's mother; that now sits in the furrows of a house, of a landscape. Their sound is a wall of righteous fertile murmurings, a gathering, a mash-up, crossed over and complicated. Sounds with no rhythm, no sequential layers – a mourning melody, I think. I hear a small girl crying. I think its Mallory. It's not. I stand beneath them. Am a part of them, but I am still standing in the glow of the morning sun, in this house, still in the world of the living. Like my mother is – only hours away from here. *Go. Go to her.*

# MOTHER

MY JEANS ARE ALL STINKING-SOUR-DAMP IN THE CROTCH. My breath like one day out from death. My armpits an itching-filth feel, and. I walk into the kitchen and grab my keys from the top of the fridge. Close the front door and run down the front stars. I am – *going* to her.

I stop beside the HQ, and. I am caught in my own image, see my reflection in the passenger-side window, see my body as larger than I have ever known it, see a collection of faint shapes surrounding me. See them. See them all there, and. I think that this could be a mirage, a daydream, a spectre of madness. See them, and. I look to my left and to my right. Look beside me, above me. They have all disappeared. I look back at the ute's windows and they have appeared again. This time their outlines are darker, their hair is moving in the soft wind. I reach out my hands and grab for them. There is nothing to hold on to. They are not here. They are not there, wherever *there* is, wherever *there* could be. Their mouths move, and I hear a soft chanting, feel their collective vibration through the souls of my feet, hear Mallory – *Cyn, go to Mum, ask her why she did it.* I open the door and jump in the ute, and. This story is so much more than just mine. It has become their collective sound of memory and loss – the stories of all the women who came before me. This is our story. Together, woven into the earth as a thick red cotton, unable to pull free and move on, and. I turn on the ignition. I put my left hand on the gearstick, put the ute into first, and. I'm driving down the dirt driveway to the front gates. Out onto the gravel, and.

IT'S AN HOUR-AND-A-HALF DRIVE THERE. It's a two-hour drive with the rain that I can hear starting to hit the roof of the ute, can see rolling down the windscreen. I'm. Driving in the opposite direction of town, turning. Right, and. Driving along State Route 48 until it grows dark. Headlights on, and. Drive. Stop on the side of the highway and piss (standing up, my pelvis out like a man), watch the bright lights from oncoming traffic shining on me as I shake and feel warm piss hit my shins, and. Half an hour left until I reach her, I see identical houses packed neatly together on the left – a new kind of suburban living. And. I'm lowering the HQ into second gear as I drive up the mountain range. Overtake a semitrailer that's struggling, and. Glide a finger over the front of my teeth to trick them into feeling clean as I reach the top. Turn right. Spray on my father's 4711 cologne, which has sat in the glove box since he left, as I put the ute back into third gear. It's still my favourite smell, all these years later. How the hell does smell have a gender? How does colour have a gender? How does pink mean your sister/best friend/mother/a woman you met at a party is having a girl? *Fucking marketing*, I say under my breath. I'm doing sixty kilometres an hour on the main street of Toowoomba, and ready for this.

AND HERE I AM. THIS IS THE PLACE. I'M READY FOR THIS. I'm slow-moving in the ute up the driveway under the fluorescent lights, between manicured lawns and past a long row of bunya pines to my left – planted with precision years ago. I'm front-end parking at an old brick building that has the word ADMISSIONS in copper lettering on the front – glass doors locked and a sign that says visiting hours aren't until morning. I'm spreading out on the cold seat and taking my boots off, with my mother only metres away. *Cyn, she's just inside.*

—

THE NEXT MORNING, I'M TAKEN TO A RECREATION ROOM in a building called the Brown House, in a ward with three doors to be unlocked to get into it. A male nurse who's dressed in all white asks me to sit and wait for my mother on a blue plastic chair, and there's. A table for games to my left. A television built into the wall in front of me. What looks like soft kids' toys in wooden boxes to my right. Just like the movies, I think. (I think of Jack Nicholson screaming, *Creeps, lunatics, mental defectives,* as Danny DeVito sits smiling and looking up at him like he's a hero.) I hear a buzzer. A door being pushed. See. My mother walking slowly towards me. My mother. She's walking towards me, looking everywhere but at me, and. I sit still as the nurse puts another blue plastic chair across from me. Tells her to sit. Walks over to the wall and leans against it. Stands watching. *There's no touching, ladies. Understand?* I look over at him and nod. Have no idea why we can't.

She is sitting across from me. My mother. She is. This is. This is the place. This is the space between us. She's playing with an elastic band on her wrist, twisting and pulling at it. She is stealing quick glances at me. She is in her own haze, her stoned palace, her getting place. I stare straight at her. I am. Still. I am. My mother's reflection. I am. The lines forming under her eyes, her copper-gold-rusted hair. I am her remembering. We are. Each other's skin, and. I don't say a word, and. My mother finally looks at me, takes a gulping breath. *You've put on weight, Cyn.* (I want to tell her that I am crowded with my history/her history/ the history of her mother/that of the woman I once met at a party. I want to tell her that grief is a thing you can measure.) *You don't want to be tied down with all that weight. Soon enough you won't fit in bus seats to get anywhere.* She laughs softly, starts rattling off a list of the things she misses in here – moisturiser, fresh meat, proper pillows, the feel of dirt under her feet, the sound of Mallory and I telling each other stories of what we were going to be when we grew up. Me. She reminds me that I was going to be a biologist when I grew up. I am certain she doesn't know what Mallory wanted to be. I stare at her hands, her white, red-freckled hands, shaking. She doesn't know how to deal with my silence. *You know what I love in here, though, love?* I lean in to her, wait for her to tell me everything. I stare at her moving mouth. Open, wide-open in her discomfort. *Confined, crowded spaces, love. The sound of the other women close to me, the polished concrete on the floors,* Oprah *and* The Jerry Springer Show *on the telly. Love, I also kinda like the idea that you might miss me. Am I right?* I place my head in my hands. Breathe deeply. *Why did you come, Cyn?* She gets up to come to me. The nurse slams the palm of his hand on the wall as a warning. *I just wanted to know why you did this, Mum – why you killed her. That back room. Those men. The knives. Mum, the fire. Why?* She slumps back down in her chair, her energy slowing, and. I mouth my sister's name three times. (I will keep saying her name forever – incantations of her.) My mother is a drug-heavy sigh. My mother is shoulders dropping into clear water – and she will never give me the answers I need. My mother is starting to cry, and. I close my eyes and listen. (Sandy shot her husband to death after years of abuse – the judge told her she was just plain crazy when he sent her here. Jolene drank so much to block out her pain that it caused psychosis – she doesn't know what's real and what isn't anymore. Marla is a risk to herself and her children – needs to be here for at least six months to sort herself out. My mother – she killed Mallory with a knife to the heart as they sat on her bed drawing pictures and talking to ghosts. My mother. She wrapped her child in a heavy blanket and walked down our front steps cradling her, laid her in the pile of dead trees. My mother. She lit the match. My mother. She stood watching.) I open my eyes and see my mother with tears rolling down her cheeks. *You hear them too, don't you, Mum?* Her mouth is full of dry-gummed ash and it opens in slow-drawl recall. *I used to, love. I did. But not after. Not after. They stopped straightaway that night. Took off. Disappeared. Poor little Mallory, poor little girl in the fire.* My mother's head lowers to her chest. Her body an exhaustion, a relief, a dazed sorrow. The nurse sees this and walks towards her, pulls her up from her chair, holds her now-languid body upright as another nurse comes in to help him take her away. They all move towards the door without a word. My mother's feet stumbling is the last thing I hear. My mother, I am nothing like her.

# SWALLOWING THE GOLD-TAPESTRIED TERRAIN

I AM SITTING IN THE HQ OUTSIDE ADMISSIONS, gasping for air, my nose running. I am watching the sky, black-blue-grey layers stirring, as I start the ute, and. I drive. Out of the driveway, up the main street, down the mountain range, and. I'm on the highway and driving into a thick blanket of the celestial sphere. I'm a woman from the dry outback who should be celebrating the oncoming torrential rain and mourning the floods that will probably hit home – a temporary relief and gratifying in the moment. My chest feels tight, constricted, like someone is sitting on top of me, their hot breath close to my ear. I hear a female voice that has a slight stutter. *Sh-sh-she, your mother, sh-sh-she never understood. Sh-she knows she got it wrong – killing your sister.* Drive.

Up the highway towards home, as. Lightning cracks open the sky, and I feel like I am sitting in a dark porcelain jar that's fallen off the kitchen bench. I am surrounded by wild-cracked fluorescence (*Cyn, sweetheart, turn off the kitchen light. You know the bugs think it's the moon. They'll just keep circling around the bloody thing all night confused if you don't turn it off when you're finished in there*). I count aloud as the air collapses and expands back in on itself above me – *one, two, three* . . . I hear their clamorous thunder, their heels, their elbows, their hips pounding – uproarious and wild like a group of Spanish dancers. (I remember my mother telling me when I was younger and hiding under the table, scared of the thunder and lightning after years of drought, listening to sounds that I'd never heard before, that thunder was *all the people who have died and gone to heaven stamping their feet and dancing.* That storms were *a party for those departed.* The rain, *expensive champagne spilt from glasses.* The lightning, *a lighter striking the smoke held by a beautiful woman,* her dress *a sequined coral-pink.*) I try to imagine them all up there as I hit one hundred and twenty kilometres an hour and listen to the low thunder as the beating heart of a young woman; imagine them together as a group of women caught in some grand Gatsby-esque vision, a glitter-banged-bliss. I try. I can't. Another sky-crack lightning

169

strike – *one, two* . . . a monstrous boom of thunder. I am in it now. The centre. At its core, and forty-five minutes out from home. I try, but I can only think of that night back then. Of the dark and heavy-set-deep-set-so-close-we-could-nearly-touch-them clouds rolling towards my father and me standing on our front steps after the cops left. Of his hands shaking in his pockets as the thunder raged in fury, as the thunder vexed, as the thunder shook the house. Of his lips opening as the first drops of rain hit his face. His head lifting up to the sky and whispering Mallory's name as the thunder seethed in recognition, of. Our loss, of. Our fetid mess. The boom, a collective anger. The rumble, as the building, the swelling, as the thigh-high vibrations forming circles of tight air all around us, and. I remember thinking back then, that night, as the rain drenched us, that heaven might not even be a place like my mother said, after all.

THE RAIN WASHES DOWN, falling in diagonal sheets as I pass a service station only twenty minutes away from home. I can't see the road in front of me. Drive. Keep driving. Slower now, and another ten minutes until I pull the HQ over next to a deep ditch on the side of the road, the kind my grandparents were found in so many years ago. I sit and wait for the rain to stop, turn the radio on to listen for the news, and. It's full of siren sounds and a warning for those a hundred kilometres north of here to pack the car, grab the kids, the dog – *leave.* (Photos and jewellery don't give much pleasure to the dead, I think.) This isn't going to stop anytime soon, and I sit surrounded by a yawning-slow black, can't see my own hands in front of me, fumble above to turn the light on. I sit. I listen to the whooping sounds of irregular air around me, to a cluster of circular movement in the heavy clouds pushing against the Earth's rotation. Spin. Spin. Spin. A violent rally. (Think of the names of storms, of cyclones. Kate. Megan. Olga. Tracey. Nora. Tiffany. Tasha. Think of what they are said to be as they approach – temperamental in nature, flirting with the coastline, teasing the town. Think about what they really are – big, bold, wild, powerful and able to destroy you. Batten down your windows, blokes. Bring the car in under the house. Go to the smallest room. Get in the bathtub. Move under a mattress. Stockpile food for when the electricity fails. Spin. Spin. Spin.) I lean over and turn down the radio, feel my breasts sagging (not long now until they become a burdened heft, until my stomach grows to act as a ledge for them to rest on – my body slower than it has ever been before, my inner arms, as I drive, sore-rubbing against my sides). I smell terrible. My hands shake. Hail starts to hit the ute – a metal blow, a mighty metal blow, and. A large piece of hail hits the side mirror nearest my head, smashes it into a million tiny pieces. (In the reflection my face is breaking apart.) The ute feels as if it is being lifted slightly off the road and the light turns on and off, on and off. On.

The hail sounds like gunfire around me. Water rises, the road now flooded around me for as far as I can see. I hear the sound of a woman sighing. A woman coughing; gasping at all the air. I hear gurgling, a woman drowning, her lungs acting as a sponge. (Gargling warm salt water from a metal cup gets rid of blisters – an old wives' tale my father used to tell me), and. I wonder if Mallory ever felt our mother's love, as water rolls down the front console and onto my knees. I see water coming in through the closed passenger-side window. I think of Mallory's smooth-young-so-near-to-light-pink skin and wonder what route her tears took on her body after they ran down her face. I think of my mother, and wonder what her face was like after she was taken from the hospital's recreation room this morning, if it had lines as dry rivers for tears, if she had great deep oceans under her eyes where the water sat, if her neck turned into a sinking wetland. (Sit next to your mother, if you are one of the lucky ones who has one near, and look closely at her face. Where have her tears passed over or furrowed in her skin? What made her tears fall? Was it a sharp slap across the face, was it feeling like she was misplaced her whole life, was it the doctor who didn't understand? Where have her tears landed, pooled? Does your mother have heavy indentations in her chin, her upper lip, in her lap? Does she have breasts which show stretch marks as rivers that widen at the nipple as their ending?) I move my hands over and down my legs to my boots. I undo my shoelaces. I take off the boots, peel off my socks. I feel with both hands the deep indents on the tops of my feet, and know that they are from the tears that have fallen while I was looking down at the earth, looking for Mallory. Small parts of her. Smells of her. A handprint, a bone. Dirt under my nails, digging. My fingers move over the indents on both my feet, and I think of the places on the map that those women above me have come from, hear a woman with a Cambodian accent, think of her country – the shape of it is like a fat old woman begging. (Open an atlas and try to work out the shape of each country. Iceland is a puffer fish. Sri Lanka is a teardrop. Finland is a flamenco dancer. The whole world above us is a cat playing with the ball that is Australia.) And I know that these women aren't part of some great Gatsby-esque party, like my mother once told me. There is no heaven-like party at which they all celebrate the lives they once lived. There are no cocktails, no laughter – sequins and glitter are reserved for the delighted. They have come together above me in anger at my mother's misreckoning, her wilful ignorance of everything they told her. They are saying over and over again through the heavy beat of the rain: *You know who we are.*

There is a deep grumble in the clouds, and. They are spreading out over the whole land before me. They are the sky as a hundred different shades of black swallowing the gold-tapestried terrain. They are every woman's name you have ever heard, and. They are able to kill large groups of us. They come over coastlines and wipe out small towns. They are a reckoning. For. Your hand on the back of her throat. For. You ignoring the woman crying on the street corner. For. You telling your daughter she is unlovable. You. Laughing at the fat woman at the gym whose stomach is escaping her leggings as she runs on the treadmill. The 'hilarious' rape joke you tell your mates. It's. You telling a woman to be quiet. It's. Touching her lightly on her breasts to confuse her into thinking that it didn't really happen. It's. Walking too close to her at night when she is nearly home. It's. The time you didn't call the cops on the next-door neighbour beating her, the time you hit her, the time you excluded her from your party, your group, your conversation, the way your father taught you to show a woman who's boss. Burrow. Embrace. Huddle. Hold. Hands firm. Arms linked. They are my/your/our reckoning, and. I wonder if my ending is as inevitable as my sister's was out here. Their noise above, is. A rolling moan. Is. A deep bellow. A breaking bang. The land creaking beneath us all. Their collective sound able to break the bonnets of cars and flood great plains, to destroy men's livelihoods, crash down ceilings in bars and unnerve those living without regret or sorrowful knowing in their actions. Their noise is the holocaust for our collective anguish, I think. A warning for all. And – *Mallory, Mallory, Mallory*, her name a soft-lipped opening – *Mallory*. She must be in these sounds, I think. She must be somewhere.

I tilt my chin up to the ceiling of the HQ. I listen harder. I try to find that known pitch of her, that slight lisp on the letter Z of her. Zebra. Zipper. Zone. Zero. I am waiting for her to say one of these words (a night-time game – my grandmother's old dictionary and a torch under the blankets, she read out each word). I wait. I see long-cracked silver flashing in the sky, hear the splitting of wood, the crash, the racket, the fall of heavy branches. I see smoke and a scar ripped down the length of an ironbark tree; its brilliant red-brown centre the exact same colour as the lines drawn across a map of Spain I once saw in the local doctor's surgery, marking the pilgrims' trails. I think of my sister's first steps, think of my mother's imagined steps in all the other places she could have gone, her walking a trail that had no real starting point and a definite end. *You should really do it*, the doctor said to my mother when he saw her looking at the lines on the map. *It will change your life.*

The water around me starts to rush away into all the crevices of the land. (*Look, girls, the land is thirsty,* my mother said as we stood at the lounge room window and watched heavy blankets of rain coming towards us. The afternoon heat breaking, that rare wonderful relief. *The land is drinking all the tears from the sky.*) Drink it all away. Drink, and. The sky becomes a sudden pale blue, a quick disappearing act above me, and. I see a rusted sheet of tin lying to the left, a cow sheltering beside a rock, an old rotten tree trunk beside a pothole. The land still. The land firm, defiant, and. There is a silence never heard. A black hole, a yawning void of mute-stillness, the aftermath of women's fury laid out before me. I sit in the calm and imagine what my own Ivy might have looked like, remember what Mallory used to feel like in my arms and imagine her rivers of tears as the last of the rainwater now running down the windscreen. (An estuary: where the river meets the sea.) I imagine that my heart is an ocean.

I open the door and step out, the mud oozing between my toes. The back tyres are stuck in the softening ground, and I lower my knees, my hands, my left ear – half my face is now a red, muddy mess. I listen for them. One whispers, *We love you.* I try to place the voice. I don't know it. I stay kneeling under our shared cerulean sky and wait for more. (Is Mallory there? Will she be louder than the rest of them?) I am. Here for a long time, longer than a sane woman should be, and. I look out over the land that is mine/ours/your mother's/your best friend's/the woman's you met one night at a party, and I think of my mother's confusion, her ignorance. I hold my hands in front of my face, see her hands, feel a burning heat on my forehead – that bloody knife.

I GET BACK IN THE HQ and sit at the steering wheel for a long time, longer than a sane woman would. It is all long time out here. I feel the dripping of mud down my neck, feel it run down between my breasts (where head-bending tears end for so many women), turn the key in the ignition and hear the motor cough and splutter. I turn the key again and it starts. I accelerate (*Just gently, love, that's all you need to get the momentum up, to set the wheels spinning. That's it. There you go*). The ute moves. I drive slowly, the road a sliding-slippery mess of oceanic potholes and large branches. Keep driving. Past a new postbox, and. Remember walking along, holding my mother's letter, holding it up to the light to try to see what she had written. (*Post this for me on your way to school, Cyn. Don't tell your father. Here's two dollars to buy yourself something special at the tuckshop.*)

I AM. EIGHTY KILOMETRES AN HOUR. I am. Driving over a ridge and around the corner. I am. At the front gates to our home. I'm driving down the dirt driveway and around the bend, looking at what has always been – our house, unchanged after all these years, so bright white against the landscape. Driving towards it. I am, each metre. I am, out of the ute and each step to her. To that spot. To Mallory. She is still here. She is, was, a finger-painted picture just for me, a plate full of sliced fruit she didn't like, a bracelet made from string, a lizard that gave her germs. And I am now, standing in the large puddle in front of our house, the place that will forever hold water when rain falls (she never did learn to swim), the place that will forever sink into itself in sadness at what it once was witness to. I think of puddles building to lakes, lakes bursting into rivers, rivers flowing out to vast sad-storied oceans. I see my reflection beneath me in the water, see the sun above me as fire. I want to lift up on my tippy-toes, bend my legs ready and dive in. Go to her. Mallory, only Mallory, and. The sun is a heated memory on my body as I unzip my jeans, push them with my underwear to my ankles and step out of them. I unbutton my shirt and take it off. I undo my bra; it falls into the water, and. I am standing there with my chest up to them all, naked. I am witness to them. That fiery sun, that beating on my chest. I am incandescent. I am luminous. I am the bravest of imaginings. I hear them like my mother does, like you might, like the woman you met one night at a party tells you she does when she is high. I am radiant, and. I am not of faint heart or uncourageous living (don't believe the lies; you'll be taught to block it all out from an early age – stay strong). I will not ignore them or think of them as something else (my intuition, my gut, my waters). Their sounds, their voices, will not be my silent undoing like my mother allowed them to be. I am not my mother, and.

# I DON'T BELONG HERE

CYNTHIA. My name, Cynthia, my mother once told me, came from Greek mythology; meant that I was born on a great mountain. When she told me this I was looking up and out through the kitchen window to the large mountain beyond the edge of our property, and I asked her if I was born there. Up there. A place higher than I had ever been before. She pointed to the lounge room and said, *No, love, you were born right there on the floor. You made a bloody mess all right.* She came in close, pressed her nose to mine and said, *Darling, you don't belong here.*

THREE

# BUT I AM SO LIKE HER

AT SIX A.M. THE PHONE RINGS. I get out of bed and walk into
the hallway where the phone sits on the wall. Pick it up. Put
it to my ear. Gladys, the boss's secretary, asks me if I'm able to
come back a day early, if I want a double shift to make up for
the money that I've lost over the last week. *Yes.* I tell her that the
rain has stopped out this way now, and she sighs and says that
it's a hard type of life for us single women out here. I sigh back
at her. (Sighs, looks, half-laughs and tears shared between us
all across this country.) I hang up and think of sticking my
knife into the heavy flesh of a half-dead beast as a release, as a
motion to move my grief along. (Can grief move from one body
to another like they tell us madness and illness can? From the

touch of a mother's hands on you, from the blood of a beast up your gloved arms, from your own baby as a tiny death in you before you get to meet her, or passing other women on the street with broken ribs, with bruises on their backs – a stomach full of stiches that nobody can see?)

AS I TURN INTO THE ABATTOIR'S CAR PARK, I see the boys are standing in a huddled group looking at something. I park the ute and climb out, hope to get past them without them noticing me, without a *whore*, or *bitch*, or *cunt* – my head down and walking quickly. I feel in my bag for my boning knives and run the edge of my thumb ever so lightly over one of the blades. (Men, think about how many times you have seen a woman in front of you on a darkened street walking quickly, how a woman crosses the road when she sees you, when a woman casually reaches for her phone to talk to someone who is probably not even there. Know that we are marvels in our deception and in our fear.) I've nearly reached the back door when Cameron sees me and smiles. *Hey, Cyn, long time no see, eh?* He starts laughing. He's the only one who does. His fearless mouth, his deep bellowed sound, is a warning to me that he is unafraid of the repercussions of their grouped violence (who'd believe the daughter of a crazy whore, I think, who would – *Cyn, love, best to keep things to yourself* – who?). A bloke named Trent clears his throat (yeah buddy, that's your sound I heard in the coldroom wasn't it? – good to put a face to it I suppose), and looks down at the ground. His brother Phil starts to pick something off his jeans that no one else can see (I wonder if they've spoken together about what they did to me). A new bloke that Cameron calls Andy fumbles with his Zippo and drops it on the ground. Laughs nervously as he bends down to pick it up, his head lifting slightly to take a quick glance at me. The four of them are floundering before me in their shame, of. What they are, of. Knowing the kinds of acts their daughters and wives are afraid of. As I push open the back door of the abattoir, Cameron yells after me, *Cyn, check out what's on the tearoom table.*

ON THE TEAROOM TABLE, between an empty can of Coke and a pile of *Picture* magazines (*don't make a fuss about it, love – the blokes love doing the crosswords*), the local newspaper is opened to a page with a large colour photo of George, his pants up high and his nipples showing from under his thin white shirt. The headline reads:

LOCAL MAN DEAD IN CAR CRASH
Local larrikin and man about town, George Michelides (73) was pronounced dead at the scene after his car veered off Bushmans Road and crashed into one of the region's

oldest bottle trees in the early hours of Sunday morning. It is believed that he suffered a major heart attack as he was driving a youth home from the all-ages disco held at Jerry's arcade. The youth was treated at the scene for bruising. Mr Michelides is survived by his wife Dot, a local Rotary and CWA member. Mrs Michelides was unavailable for comment.

Beneath the colour photo is a black-and-white picture of George and a girl in front of Jerry's arcade (*stretch that arsehole nice and wide, sweetheart, just like your mother used to*). The old bastard has a massive cheque for five hundred dollars in his hands and is about to give it to her. Surrounding them is a group of young girls in matching bright yellow t-shirts sitting on their bikes. Everyone is smiling, and I can just make out in the background those seats in the back-corner booth, a group of young men playing pool, and that back door – locked.

Cameron walks into the tearoom. As he stands at the sink filling a glass with water, he turns to me and smirks. I stare back at him until he becomes uncomfortable in the quiet between us (hold your silence, your place – hold), says to me after he's finished drinking, *No more young pussy for old George now, eh, Cyn?* (*I am not my mother. I am not my mother.* I say it over and over again in my head.) He walks out of the room laughing.

—

BEHIND THE METAL TABLE in the cutting and boning room, the hard plastic bench I'm standing at is full of knife lines and dents. (Fucking amateurs, I think to myself every time I stand in front of it, the rubber mat beneath my feet making sounds with the blood that gets caught under it. Fucking amateurs – a thin knife right through the leg, a clean-lined knifing to the hide. Two neat motions are all it needs.) Across from me, I watch Thuy, Maggie and Kim awkwardly slicing muscle from bone. They are like a coven in here: a squad, a gang, a terror – their shared history and origin holding them together, their foreign tongue as their refuge. (Without the rest of us holding on to each other with our histories, how do we come together, how to we hold on and keep strong?) Together, they lean towards me as one and ask with their hands waving blood in the air and half-syllables coming from their mouths, why I haven't been to work. *Men,* I say, gesturing around me – *bad men.* My hands dropping to my sides in defeat. They give me a knowing *Ahhh,* nod and go back to their animated conversation that will never include me.

I stand for hours, my legs sore and my hands cramping. (*Drop the knife, shake your hands out, flick your fingernails to stop the ache.*) David, who lost his wife to cancer last year, wraps the fresh meat in thick plastic ten metres down the line, yells at us at random intervals that we are going too fast for him to keep up, and. I push a mound of fat off the bench and into the bin beneath me as the foreman stands at the door with a smoke in his mouth and watches us work. Above him, one of the air-conditioner units looks like it's about to fall on him – it hasn't been fixed in months.

At six that night I leave my knife on the sharpening stone and walk out to the basins, take off my gloves and hang them up on the hooks, wash my aching hands with the lemon-scented soap. *I need a fucking smoke*, I mumble to myself, walking up the hall and pushing my way through the stained and heavy plastic curtains, opening the back door. I walk alone under the growing moonlight to the back of the sheds and sit down on the ground under an old fluorescent light that doesn't work anymore. I take a smoke out of the packet and light it (fire in the lungs, fire in the lungs), remember the day I brought my grade seven schoolbook home at the end of term for my mother, the gold sticker on the front shining in the afternoon sun. *You shone so brightly out there*, my mother said to me as I walked into the kitchen, her soapy gloved hands lifting up out of the sink as she turned to face me.

THE BELL SOUNDS. Smokes stubbed out. Coffee cups left on the bench. Gloves on. We all get back to work. (A collective bend in our backs, the job of killing the living weighs heavy on us, and the longer you work here the more pronounced the bend.

Pat didn't even look up anymore, couldn't, his neck bent so low that you had to lean down just to hear what he said.)

I'm back at my cutting bench. (A second shift. A second shift. Shake your hands and keep on going.) I'm picking up the largest knife and running it under water, holding it up in front of my face, and. It reflects the cracked and yellow fluorescent lights above me, reflects my own face back at me (my nose, my eyes, the heavy bags of skin under them, my full set of chipped teeth). I. See my mother's reflection as my own, hear her yawn. I. Slam the knife into the breastbone of a beast, feel tears fall down my cheek and wonder how many of my tears would have to fall to fill a bucket, a bath, a backyard swimming pool. I think about how much weight is carried in storm clouds, how much is held in oceans about to break into tidal waves and floods. I think of the heavy sound around my mother's temples, in her ears, at her forehead. I touch my stomach and feel the weight of my own body, so much heavier than it was last year. My pants so tight it's hard to sit in them. Each work day for weeks now, a few sausage rolls and a chocolate milk from the pie truck for morning tea, a packed lunch, and. On the way home a visit to the corner store – a large white paper bag of musk sticks (my mother used to call them chalk lollies), freckles and milk bottles. A handful of Golden Roughs and a cola Sunnyboy for the drive home. I rip open the top of the Sunnyboy pyramid and taste the foil lining between my teeth, start sucking out all the sweet goodness from the ice as soon as I start the car. Feel the sugared freeze setting in. That high, and. By the end of each night, I've eaten all the lollies and don't feel a thing. That numbing. That dull. That stunned fog I know so well. I think that grief is a weight that we all carry in different ways. My back aches. I slice. Cut. Push with my elbows down on the beast to get it right. Blood running to the front of the bench. My ankles ache. I listen as the men standing on the platform above us hang fresh carcases on hooks and talk about how good of a bloke George was. *Champion. Legend. Always a handshake when he saw us.* A few of them glance at me, and then quickly look away.

STANDING AT the metal wash basin at the end of my shift, I take off my gloves, press soap into my hands and wash my arms, elbows, scrub under my fingernails. I take my shoes off and shake out the heated blood. Peel off my socks. (*No, we won't be putting doors on the showers, just bloody jump in, woman. You're the only one in here who doesn't.*) My toes are all wrinkled and soft, and I start to walk barefoot with the boots in my hand up the walkway to leave for the day (*and put your bloody boots on. You know you can't walk around like that in here*). Coming towards me is a group of men, laughing. When they see me, they shut up, stop in their tracks, part and move to each side of the walkway, their backs up against the walls and their hands behind their backs, looking down at the ground. They are scared of me, I think, scared of what I could do, what I could say, what my mother did to Mallory, of all the things that they choose to leave unspoken.

AN HOUR AND A HALF LATER I'm standing in my towel with my hair dripping wet and looking down: at the glossy, the scratchy, the thickly, thinly, largely, the small, the ephemera from my mother, still scattered on the lounge room floor. I bend down to start cleaning it up, and. Wonder how I can get the inked bruise out of the wood. It is the colour that bruises turn when they heal, and. I remember the huge one on my thigh that day after I fell off my BMX, when I was trying to do a bunny hop to impress my father. I was so fascinated by the colours of the bruise changing each day after. *Look, Dad, it's getting darker, it's getting worse.* Then, a few days later, becoming excited when the colours matched the pictures of solar systems and stars in my science books at school. And, I remember how troubled I was when I realised that it was finally turning the same brown colour as the land, turning the yellow shades of the long dry grass near the front gate. My body, which I'd thought might belong in faraway galaxies, was in fact just part of the earth surrounding us.

Kicked under the dining room table is a folded-up piece of paper, and I get down on my hands and knees to grab it. I stand back up and open it, place my fingers on the red-burnt-orange-yellow of lines, all grouped together in the middle of the page like a brilliant burning star. There was never going to be any other ending for us, I think. Fire, bright booming fire as my mother's avowed anger at my father for leaving her in a place where she didn't belong, her final act a release from the pressure of all those women's voices in her head that she didn't understand. I run my fingers through my wet hair and cup my hand to my mouth, smell my sour breath as metallic-rusted blood, feel the air change around me. Feel it, as. Soft cushions, as. Heavy blankets, as. My mother holding me in her arms, to. Stepping into a warm bath. *Cyn.* I hear Mallory at my chest. *Cyn.* I feel my own unborn daughter, Ivy, between my legs. *Cyn.* I think of Simon whispering in my ear at Jerry's arcade, telling me that he loved me. I hear George grunting at the back of my head, those men in the coldroom with their pants to their ankles. *Urgh. Whore. Hummp.*

I AM SO LIKE MY MOTHER. The way she held the knife. I am the slamming of blades in the backs of near-dead beasts. I am. The way her hips swayed as she walked, my shadow on the lounge room walls as her own. I am looking down, one foot in front of the awkward other as I walk to the kitchen. I am the smooth

mountains of my own name. *Cynthia. Great mountains.* I am.
Her flaming hair. I am pulling strands of it out. I am. The
memory of her held by others. I am a whore/cunt/slut/take-it-
like-you-fucking-love-it to men who know no better. I am not
her confusion, I am not her enclosure, her set place on the map.
I am not her imaginings, her madness, her meeting men at the
front door late at night and walking them down the hallway,
thinking that her daughters couldn't hear a thing. *I am all grand
fucking possibility*, I say out loud. I am the way forward, a new
home. I am you/us/your mother/your best friend/the woman
you met one night at a party. I am every one of you who knows
she is more than this.

Walking into the back room. I am. Pulling down all her dream
catchers, all her clothes off the rack. Pulling out her drawers.
Ripping her pillows apart with my teeth. I am. Under a soft
shower of polyester filling, and stepping onto her bed, pulling the
long piece of fishing line and cut black ribbon off the wall – my
fingers prickling with the pressure. I grab armfuls of her things
and carry them to the front verandah, throw them all over the
railing onto that spot, that forever hollow spot. I am. Making
a mountain to burn. I am twenty-three steps each time I walk
back to her room for more. I am stamping on the photo of her.
How much more was there to understand? I think of the things
that knives could cut: envelopes, tins, packages, plastic bottles.

I think of things that knives could do: break open boxes, break open a beast, break open my sister's skin. I think of knives cutting the bandages of the wounded, slicing down the length of a cucumber, ripping open the base of the mattress.

THAT NIGHT I STAND BY THE FIRE PIT drinking some of my father's old whisky. I light a match. I light two. I throw them on her things. The fire comes to life, blazes violently with roaring sound.

# A MAD KIND OF LONGING

GRIEF IS A CIRCLE, a whirlwind, a never-ending, no ending, will it ever end, all wrapped up in memory-churn. *Come, Cynthia.*

I put on my mother's black dress with the red flowers. (*Polyester, Cyn, it's the best kind of fabric to wear out here – it dries quick when you get all sweaty. But bloody hell it's hard to get rid of your own smell in it.*) I hold Mallory's favourite toy, Bunchy, under my arm. I am driving to the abattoir and smelling the scent of bleach, warm blood, rusted-on carnage as I arrive. I am parking and nodding to a group of men in bloodied overalls smoking near the back door. I am walking straight to the bush. One hundred and sixty-seven steps to the edge of it. I am ready as the rising sun streams through the tight cluster of trees. Gold-dusted land. Ambered leaves drying on the ground. I am one step in front of the other. I see the long arm of a woman reach up towards the canopy of the trees. I hear the giggles of two old women who look the same. I see a baby undressed under a fallen branch with a distorted lip, one eye a different colour from the other. Fourteen more steps, and there is a group of women standing, their bare bottoms forming a circle (a cushion for pushin', money maker, a tail – why can't we just call parts of a woman's body what they actually are, eh?). The women are holding hands, and. Another step as one of them turns to me, her low-hanging breasts looking like they have been mauled by the claws of a tiger. Blood seeps down her stomach and into her crotch. I hear my own breath come out of my mouth as audible fear, hear her say, *It's okay, dear, Mallory has told us all about you.* My breath stops. Two hundred and five steps to hear her name. No one but me has said her name aloud for years. (How do we keep the names of our dead with our living? I wonder. Is it just in books and art? How do we keep our sounds, our stories with us? How do we hold on to each other and link arms with our mother's mother, with her mother, with hers, with the beginning – with the mother of us all? I remember when my father told me about the original people of this land. He said that they knew how to hold on to and share their stories, that their connection to this land, their land, was the key to it all – every rock, every tree, every creek. The Dreaming, he said they called it.) Ten more steps, and. I am standing in front of an old woman. She smells of rotten fish and something sweet like overripe fruit. I wonder what happened to her, why she smells so strongly – a fall in a river, a push? Was she left in a place where others wouldn't find her? Was she buried in the middle of an apple orchard? Did she just get lost, unable to find her way home? *Come*, she says. *Come*, they all say together. The circle opens up for me and I step inside it. The circle closes. There is a soft hum now, like live powerlines all around me, like the beat that sits under songlines, or as horrid silences between fighting lovers, of young bodies resting after fucking – each beat as a biography. Standing in the centre, I turn around, looking at each of them. There are probably seventy women, eighty, ninety; there are others in the trees and hidden in the bushes. I stop turning and they all drop their hands to their sides, smile at me. Stare at me. *Where is she?* I ask. *Where is she? Why isn't she here?* I feel heat building under my feet. They don't answer. *Mallory*, I call, feeling the soles of my feet throb in time with the beating hum of the women. *Mallory, I know you're here, sweetheart*, I scream at the trees. The women join hands again and start moving in a slow circle around me; chanting names, dates, times, seasons, a list of natural disasters like they are reading from a guidebook that is mapping their misplacement. The trees move and sway around us, and. I am certain I can hear Mallory beneath me.

Falling to my knees, I start running my hands through the loose dirt, start crawling through it to find her. *I will dig all the way to the other side of the Earth for you, Mallory,* I yell. I say it again, placing my ear to the ground and looking up at the women around me – at their legs, arms, broken noses, lost hair, and. Different shapes, sizes, beautiful, plain and ugly. I stand with them in their damaged states, in their sadness, their release, in their comfort. I lift my head up, keep moving my hands through the dirt as the sounds of incantations circle around me, and. Gold. Gold flecks catch my eye and I move my hands over the glinting colour. Gold dust. Gold sun. Golden leaves around me. Small gold circle. It's Mallory's other earring, and I feel with my left hand the matching one now hanging around my neck on the end of a gold chain, remember the feel of it rolling around in my mouth, my tongue pushing it over my top teeth, over my bottom teeth. *Where are you, Mallory?* I scream into the bush as I hold the second earring between my fingers. I get up and walk, break open the joined hands of two blonde, tanned women, and start searching for her. I peer under large rocks. I pick up small ones. I move my feet through large mounds of leaves and move my arms and legs like a snow angel in others. I climb trees and push large palm fronds out of the way. I look behind stumps, trees, find a group of girls playing in the hollow of a tree trunk and think one of them is her. I grab at her from behind, and she turns to me, her eyes filling with tears when she realises that I am not the mother she's been waiting for.

As night comes, as night falls, as night turns the ground beneath us all into a carpet of soft-mossed rolling swell, I sit building and burning effigies of golden leaves for her, say her name over and over, join in with the chorus of chanting all around me – *Mallory*, and. The women around me start to hug each other in farewell, kiss each other on the shoulders, on the cheeks, on the places where they have been hurt, and move away for the night. There are lips pressed on the forehead of a woman whose hair has been pulled from her skull, on the arm of an old woman who seems to have had it bent back in shapes that are unnatural for the living. As the last woman is about to leave, she asks me for my hand, leads me to two shrubs of lemon-scented tea tree that have been uprooted. Their thin coppery leaves give way to the darkest green on their tips. *Have these*, she says as she picks up both shrubs and places them in my arms. *Take them home with you and surround yourself with our comfort. They'll start throwing off white flowers soon, if you look after them right.* She holds me close and whispers into my ear that this isn't a place where the living should stay for longer than they need to, that those who do succumb to a strange kind of thinking. My fingers move over the rising fleshy marks on her wrists as I thank her, and.

As I walk towards the lights of the car park, I notice an older woman who I've seen in town occasionally, sitting at the edge of the bushland with her ear to the ground. She looks up at me as I approach but she doesn't move. *Shhhhh*, she says in a low whisper. *Shhhh – don't say a word. I think I've just heard her.* I ask her who she is listening for. *My one love*, the woman says, her hands trembling on the ground beside her head. *Her husband found out about us. She knew he would kill her if he did. Shhhhhh, I think that's her.* She turns her head and places her other ear on the ground, moves again and places her mouth close to the earth and says, *Darling, can you hear me? It's me. It's Dianne.* I walk away, leaving her to her own kind of mad longing.

CAMERON, PETER, JIM, A NEW GUY I'VE NOT SEEN BEFORE, all working a night shift in the slaughtering shed and now standing beside my ute on their break. Lately, there's been talk of Cameron purposefully leaving cattle waiting in the stun box for longer than he should. *A beast waiting in there can smell the blood in the shed, love,* Pat told me on my first day. *They're not bloody stupid. Only a cruel fuck would do a thing like that. And there's plenty of 'em here. You'll find out soon enough.* As I'm walking up to the HQ with my arms full of shrubs, I see they're all smoking and drinking cartons of chocolate milk bought from the pie van earlier in the day. They turn around, and the new guy walks towards me and asks me if I'm okay. Before I can answer, he tells me his name is Johnno, and he grabs the shrubs out of my arms, tells me he'll put them in the back of the ute for me. *Good luck growing these things anywhere but in there*, he says as he lifts them into the tray. *At least you didn't pay for 'em, eh.* I look at myself in the ute's window and see dirt covering my face, see my hair as a bird's nest with feathers and twigs sticking out, the top of my dress pulling down and showing off my breasts, now heavier than they've ever been. *So, the boys tell me you're single.* He places his right hand on the roof of the ute as Cameron says to him, *Leave it, Johnno, leave it. Seriously. Tainted goods.* Johnno moves his hand off the roof and half smiles at me, walks back to the rest of the men with the swagger of a young man who gave it a red-hot go. As I drive out of the car park, I look in the rear-view mirror and see him watching me leave.

# A GROVE, A TUFT, A SHRUBBERY

THE SUN IS BRIGHT THIS MORNING, and I'm sitting behind the steering wheel of the HQ. There's a line of cars before me. We all wait, as. A young man in a crisp white shirt and low-slung black pants waves his arms, telling us where to park. I nod my head and turn into a car spot when he directs me, turn off the ignition and watch people in their finest clothes walk past, behind the ute – suits not worn for years, hats their mothers bought when they were fashionable, white pearls, black high heels, dark dresses and flowers in hands. The clutched handbags. I haven't seen so many Greek people in one place together before, I think, and. I sit and watch as they walk to the front door of the church, wonder if my mother ever saw so many in the one spot when they shipped her off to live in the city all those years ago. (*Fucking greasy wogs*, my father used to say after the local mechanic came out to fix his forever-breaking-down tractor. *They're fucking invading the place.*) On the steps of the church a priest is handing out booklets with George's face on the front. It's been months since his death – his wife, I assume, not wanting a funeral (her intuition, her gut, her waters – her knowing, I bet, of his violent nature), and the priest, I guess, finally convincing her that a good Greek wife would at least have a memorial service for him.

The boys from work, from Jerry's arcade, stand in a circle (always a circle) just near the priest in their unironed shirts and with their hands in their pockets. Simon isn't with them. I let out a sigh of relief, take a smoke out of the packet as the last of the mourners pass and strike my lighter. The smoke rises, and. There he is. There is Simon. There's Simon standing behind the ute and looking straight at me. I sit still beneath the moving smoke. I look straight ahead, pretending I don't notice him in the rear-view mirror. I wish myself into ash, into a vestige – something that once was but is no longer in existence for him. He walks along the side of the ute and taps on my window. I turn slowly to face him, and we are both still and staring at each other for the longest time. (Time moves slowly. Time moves slowly until it doesn't), and. I wind down the window and wait for him to start talking. *Cyn.*

He is bending down to me. *I didn't think you'd be here, because of, well, you know. Fuck – you know.* I have nothing to say to him, there hasn't been anything to say since the day I woke up in that hospital. *I've been wanting to get in touch with you, Cyn, to, you know, see how you are. The boys tell me that you've been a bit quieter at work these days – that, well, you aren't acting like your usual self.* A small smirk starts to form on the corners of my lips, and. I look up to the rear-view mirror and notice that there is a woman sitting in his new Commodore. She's beautifully plain and she's staring at us. She's patting down loose strands of her gold-blonde hair and putting on her lipstick. She's getting out of the car. She's walking towards us. She's pregnant. Simon looks down at his shiny black shoes. *Well, it's good to see you, Cyn. I better run. Late and all that.* I watch them walk into the church together, and. I think of how beauty is determined, how the symmetrical, the smooth and the young are favoured. Like fruit, I think to myself. Like fruit – the odd shaped pieces that I always thought tasted the sweetest were thrown in the bin. I don't move from the ute. The doors of the church close. As I hear the service begin, I see a group of young girls on their bikes on the road, looking towards the church as I am, and not saying a word.

MY MOTHER'S OLD WHITE SAUCERS, the lemon-scented bushes from behind the abattoir, rusty old tins found under the house, paint once used by my father and paintbrushes sitting in a bucket of turps to make them come alive again. I'm on my knees, days after the memorial service, in my mother's back bedroom with my legs crossed, eating Vegemite on toast, surrounded by it all. It's so hot already, so early in the day, hotter than I can ever remember it being, and. I've got my mother's old togs on (Why would she need them out here? Did she swim in the ankle-shallow dams after rains hit? Did she jump in the water tanks?). I've got a spray bottle of water beside me that I'm spraying over my legs. I eat the toast slowly under the broken rays of the sun.

*Cyn? Cyn? Are you here?* I hear my name called and a heavy knock on the open front door. I hear footsteps, and there is Simon standing at the bedroom door, his knees scratched and his work boots covered in dry grass. He looks around the bedroom then bends down and picks up one of the shrubs, shakes the dirt from its roots. *So, pot plants, eh?* I nod slowly and get up, eat the last piece of toast, my breasts bursting out the sides of my mother's togs. He steps over the bucket of turps and comes towards me, asks me if I'm feeling okay. *Fine,* I say as he moves his hands towards my waist to hold me. *Looks like you're not made for those togs, Cyn.* His eyes move from my breasts and down to my growing stomach, to the thick red hairs escaping from the crotch of the togs. *Looks like you could do with a few sizes bigger and a bloody shave.* I push his hands away and feel my body move like heavy waves, walk into the bathroom and grab a towel to put around my waist. I ask him what he wants. He stands close to me, too close for a man whom I never loved, and. I can smell oil on his skin, the parched earth, another woman's faint perfume. *So*, I say, *what's the name going to be?* He steps back and looks around the crowded room. *Whose name?* he asks. I say, *The kid. Your kid. The stomach. The funeral. The woman.* (Your ripe fruit, mate.) *Oh*, he says, as he heads into the lounge room. *Oh, well I thought we might call her what you and I were going to call ours. You know, in honour of her or something. Thought you wouldn't mind.* He can't say her name, I think to myself, as he stands in the lounge room looking at the scratchy, the thickly, thinly, largely, the small. The crumpled mess now sitting on the kitchen table. *What's these then? Got a kid of your own I don't know about?* I step over the plants and the saucers, think of all the things he'll never understand. I stand behind him, stand too close. *They're my mother's*, I say to him. *Found them when I got back here.* He turns to me and starts to chuckle. *Mad, that mother of yours. I'm surprised you came back here, Cyn.* I feel heat in my stomach expanding and moving to my chest, to my neck, running all the way up to my blushing cheeks. I think of my mother now locked up in the madhouse, hear the soft rustle of the plants in the bedroom as a caution. *Suppose most blokes who used to come around here knew she was mad as a cut snake, right? 'Cept your bloody father.* I think of the faces of all the men I've ever known blending together as heat-waxed skin, of their hands as a large fleshy knot, of their chests as a deep awkward sigh. *Anyway, thought I'd pop round and check on you after seeing you at the memorial service. Cameron still jokes about what George used to do to you at the arcade. You know, I worry about you, Cyn. I tried to save you from it all – you know that, right? I still think about what we could have had.*

He gets up and starts to walk through the house, moves from room to room like a real estate agent ready for a sale. I don't move an inch, claim my own space among this. *You've really made this place cosy, haven't you?* he says, as the roof iron cracks softly under the heat of the midday sun. I feel a soft rumbling at my feet, hear a crash, a fall in the back room. In the distance I hear a truck coming down the dirt driveway. I move quickly through the house and find him standing beside my mother's bedroom window – glass broken at his feet. *Honestly, Cyn, I was just standing here and it smashed right in front of me.* He wipes blood from a small cut on his nose where it was hit by glass, and I walk up to him, my face so close to his that our noses almost touch. *Leave.* He tries to embrace me, pulls my body into his. His breath is now a heavy yearning. I pull away, I push him away. *Come on, love, I just wanted to see if you're okay out here. There's no need to be like that, is there?* He walks out of the kitchen and through the lounge room to the front door, trips over a group of potted palms on his way out.

On the front verandah we stand together and watch as the truck pulls up to the house. The truck driver waves and yells out his window to Simon. *Where do you want this lot, mate?* I point towards the ashy pit, and the driver waves in acknowledgement, smiling. He reverses the truck in, releases the back of the tray and dumps a pile of dirt. He gets out, wiping his brow with his elbow to stop sweat getting in his eyes, and takes out potted ferns, kangaroo paws, peace lilies, succulents, a small pot of delicate ivy. He places them beside the mound and gives us both the thumbs-up as he gets into the truck and drives away. Simon shakes his head as he walks down the front stairs. *You know,* I yell at him as he gets in his car, *Ivy was the name for* my *girl, not yours.* I watch him get in his car and drive off, and. I walk down the stairs and stand among the new plants, move my fingers over the softness of the kangaroo paws, hold handfuls of dirt, start to move the plants, move buckets full of dirt into the house.

LATE INTO THE AFTERNOON I pot plants in the back room, I paint old tins bright colours. I place them all as a grove, as a tuft, as a shrubbery, as a bed. A chamber. The windowsill is a reservoir of succulents. There is a soft-clapped cheering. There is an open-mouthed heat.

# HOW ABOUT AN UPRISING?
## (MAYBE EVEN A REVOLT)

BRING HER TO ME. SHOW ME. I am hours later, sitting in the middle of my mother's back room. I am sweating. I am legs shaking in the moonlight and screaming at them all around me. I am sitting on top of the pile of my mother's glossy, scratchy, thickly, thinly, largely, small, moved from the dining room table. I am, hands beside me. I am, sitting on a bed of the ephemeral – paper that will burn with the slightest spark. I watch as a redback spider moves in its own web between the fronds of monstera that I've placed near the window (so feared, but too small jawed to be effective in their inflated lore) – the heat that builds at this time of year always brings them out, I think, and. I remember my pregnant mother sitting with me on the couch one afternoon before Mallory was born. *So hot, so hot,* she said, with sweat running down her chin and down her body towards the V-shaped spot where her legs opened to let the air in, the couch sticking to her skin in the humidity. *Nothing ever moves in summer out here, not even the bloody air,* she said, as she lifted up her skirt and used it as a fan to move the air around her and into her. The heat as an exhaustion. Her feet in a bucket of water (*more ice, more ice, what do you mean we have run out of fucking ice?*), and wishing aloud for my father to come home early. (His dirt-encrusted hands so much better than my small ones at relieving the pressure at the base of her spine.) That afternoon, as I sat beside her, I felt the small whisper of something on my shin, looked down and saw a huge huntsman spider running over me, its large dark legs shocking against my pale skin. I remember hearing my own screams as I jumped up and moved my body like a tic on a dogs tail, and. My mother's laughter, her clutching her stomach, her flaming hair sticking to her chin. *That poor little thing is more afraid of you than you are of it, Cyn.* She rose like a large animal and her arms held me as I cried, rubbed my back, kissed my face. The feel of her on me. Touching me. The feel of her.

I GO TO THE FRIDGE, grab a beer and carry it out to sit on the front steps of the house, taking in the night. There are no living voices around me here. There is no mother, no father, no sister. There are no strange men coming over to fuck me. There is no travel to distant lands like my parents once dreamt of doing, no dead beasts hanging from metal hooks, or arcades with young kids drinking vodka. I scream my name into the night and wait to hear it echo. (Of course, it doesn't.) I get up and fetch another beer, and sit back on the steps with the hope that my echo has returned. (Of course, it hasn't.) It's like I don't even exist out here, like maybe I never did (like, maybe this has just been a whole dream sequence), and. I wonder, if Mallory were still alive, would we have moved or stayed here, would we have lost touch and thought of each other often, would she have travelled to different parts of the world, would our mother have been a loving grandmother, come to our weddings, attended our university graduations with our father? I light a smoke, take a deep drag and hold it in until the smoke starts to scratch my throat, to remind myself that I am, in fact, persistent in my living, that my mother was probably right on the edge of understanding hers – just a generation away from knowing. I hold my beer up to the moonlight and see the small amber bubbles floating. *She isn't mad*, I yell at the men I imagine walking up these steps to her; at my father, now living in the city, I assume; at the men standing in a circle at the abattoir. My mother isn't mad, she isn't a whore, she isn't crazy or unloved. She is the opposite of these things, the opposite of their ideas of her. My mother was in, the.

Wrong place, at the. Wrong time, and. All there is left of her out here now is a bed made of paper, and a daughter collecting effigies and conjuring up a dead girl from the land she sits on. Life becomes death becomes life becomes death – and we are all made up of fold upon fold upon folded memories. That is all there is here now. And I am not my mother. But I am so like her. Forever together in space and time, our shape still a mystery, but the folding of it, like Einstein once predicted, has created shortcuts for our long journeys across the cosmos.

INSIDE, the ivy I potted has already started to reach out for a wall in the back bedroom, will grab on and go wild in a matter of days. Women's voices begin to rise in there, begin to vibrate off the walls, their lips touching, hands holding hands holding hands. They are celebrating like a liberated army – firing shots up to the sky and kissing strangers as they dance in the centre of the room. Leaves from a maidenhair fern are scattered on the floor like confetti. I feel as though I am going to laugh, as though I am going to convulse, scream, gag. I feel like they have become me, like I have become their agent in the living world. Like a preacher, a travelling salesperson: *Have you heard about the women who once . . . Did you know that this woman . . . How many of those women do you think . . . Would you like to join our tribe, our team, our club?* I shout, *Ladies, how about we start an uprising?* (I really want you to know, that you can be an agent for us. Maybe you could find someone to talk to about this story, start building a movement with them, offer a new way? If you're brave enough, maybe you can even talk with both men and women about starting a revolution. I'll start: *watch me.*)

# HOW POWERFUL A WOMAN

I'M PULLING INTO THE VACANT LOT NEXT TO THE ORIENT HOTEL between Brisbane's CBD and Fortitude Valley. (I'm the woman you can see as you stand behind the bar looking out the window. The one who looks like she isn't from here. *Watch me, I'm glorious.*) I'm walking around the front of the hotel, looking at the gig posters pasted on the wall – Regurgitator, Six Ft Hick, a whole lot of hand-drawn posters for a goth club on the second floor, and. I'm around the corner and pushing the heavy glass door open, booking a room upstairs for the night. A man sitting alone and watching the horse races on the television turns to watch me as I say, *Thank you*, and walk up the green carpeted stairs. One flight. Two. My right hand on the wooden railing all the way up to the third floor. I'm the fourth door down. Number thirty-four. I'm unlocking the door with an oversized key. I am pushing open the door to the smell, of. Fresh paint. Carpeted ash and piss. Freshly laundered sheets. Cheap soap wrapped in thin white paper on the basin in the corner. The damp of an air conditioner that has been left on too long – such a familiar Queensland smell.

I put my bag on the bed and take out my mother's dress, still covered in dirt from the night in the bushland, and. It smells of sweat and lemons. I stand at the bathroom sink and turn on the tap, scrub the dress with soap and watch the brown water run away. I hang it on a bent coathanger I find in the small cupboard in the corner and put it in front of the air conditioner, set it on turbo mode (*polyester,* I say out loud, *dries quick).* I undress and lift my armpits up to the cool air to dry them out. Naked in front of the mirror above the basin, I smooth my mother's old foundation on my face. I rub rouge into my cheekbones with my fingertips. I smooth the brightest pink lipstick over my cracked lips – a salesperson ready to sell. My reflection is my mother's face, is her copper-gold-rusted hair, is her sky-blue eyes – high seas meeting flames. I am her body bloated and amplified from carrying the grief of all our living. My/your/our mother/your best friend/the woman you met one night at a party/the woman you've never met sits under my skin as yellowed fat, as heavy water, as clogging arteries, as a sure-fire early death. I put on a fresh bra and underwear. Put the now-dry dress on. Pull, creep, stretch it down over my body – so much tighter than it was only days ago. I pull out my mother's red high heels, which I'd found this morning in the back of my father's wardrobe (*those legs, those glorious legs,* my father said to my mother as she paraded in her new dress in front of us one night before Mallory was born), put my toothbrush, deodorant, a hairbrush on the small plastic ledge in the bathroom. Grab my wallet, my lighter. Another pack of smokes – no, grab two. Hear the women softly tapping on the window to wish me luck. Hear the sounds of a group of them jumping up and down in the toilet. The breaking of the plastic air freshener, the toilet brush. A group of them howling like I'm about to score a try at a football game. (Well-behaved women seldom make history.) And, I'm walking out of the room, down the stairs, tripping over my heels on the last step. Recover, and I'm straight into the public bar.

A WOMAN IN THE CORNER OF THE BAR SLIDES A DOLLAR COIN INTO THE JUKEBOX. She starts to sway alone in front of the small flashing lights listening to R&B. (I think of those women I've seen in videoclips wearing fluoro bike pants and sitting on young men's laps.) Her hair is an icy white, and she is head up to the ceiling, lost in the sounds of a love song. I walk over to her on my way to the bar to tell her that I love this song too. But before I reach her, she turns her back to me and closes her eyes, starts humming along with the chorus. I keep walking. Fourteen sticky steps to the bar, and. I order a XXXX. A schooner. Sit down on the tall stool and put my feet on the spittoons, full of ripped up beer coasters and cigarette butts. The barmaid looks me up and down as I settle into the seat and take a large swig of the beer. I let out a burp and don't even cover my mouth (*Cyn, be a lady. Bloody hell, if you can't leave the room to burp, at least cover your mouth*), place the schooner on the bar and look straight back at her. She's seen all this before, I'm guessing, and I smile at her, open my mouth to say something but she turns away from me with a scowl rising. She plunges her hands into the soapy-watered basin, starts washing up glasses and mumbling to herself, and. I wonder if she can hear all the women who've come before, wonder if they can be heard by others in the hum of this bar.

I sit and finish my beer. I look down the length of the bar to a group of businessmen reading newspapers and drinking bourbon and Cokes. I turn and see the woman still dancing to a love song. *A broken heart, hey,* I say to the barmaid as she puts another schooner of beer in front of me and extends her left palm to be paid. She ignores me and walks towards the men, flirts for tips.

Two young women walk into the bar, stand near me and order vodka and sodas. *Skinny bitches – you know that's what Sally calls them, right?* the taller one says to her friend. *She loves it when a barman gets all flustered when she orders one.* The women take their drinks and walk to a table near the window that has a view to the street and the bus stop, sit together laughing and looking out into the night, and. I wonder who or what they are waiting for here; they seem so impatient in each other's company. I smile at a woman in patent leather heels and a grey pants suit who joins the businessmen. I try to talk to the barmaid again – *Did you hear about that woman who . . . ?* She turns her back on me. I give up. I walk over to the woman still dancing and offer her a dollar for another song. As I stand, pulling down my dress that's creeping up and holding out the coin, she looks down at my hands and then back up at the pressed metal ceiling, throws her long peroxided hair over her shoulder and turns to sway at the wall. (How do we begin to recognise each other? Who are the ones we start to gather with? Who will listen to me when I tell them about those women floating all around us in their mystical haze?)


AN OLD WOMAN WITH MATTED HAIR walks through the door and sits down on the stool I had been sitting on by the bar. I watch as she fingers the top of my beer glass; the dark amber rings on her fingers match the colour of the liquid. She lifts the schooner to her mouth and drinks, and. She looks up at me when I walk back over, stand beside her. *Are these your smokes, love? Mind if I bum one?* I tell her I don't mind, tell her that was my beer, tell her that's my bag at her elbow. She smiles at me as I sit down and tells me her name is Hazel, as one of the businessmen from the end of the bar walks by on his way to the toilets. As he passes us, he leans in and whispers, *Hey, hey, crazy bitches*, and touches our wild hair with his fingertips. Hazel smirks at me as he does this, and makes some comment about the size of his cock as he's walking away, leans over the bar and smiles at the barmaid, buys a ticket for the next dog race to be shown on the screen above, orders another beer for each of us. Her fingers tap on the bar, and she takes a large sip of her beer, sighs out relief. *Those fuckers don't know what's coming their way*, she says to me as I light up a smoke. *One day it'll hit 'em. You know, going to a job that they hate all week, catching the same bus, eating the same goddamn packed lunches and having the same goddamn boring conversations with their slow-as-fuck workmates about the game on the weekend or the new cars they're planning to buy. They think they've got it all worked out, love.* She looks up at the screen above the bar and tells me she's been keeping her eye on a particular dog for the last few weeks, the one that's now trailing the pack. She stands up and starts to scream at the TV, slaps her hand on the bar – placing all her dreams on a win. And as the dog comes in fifth, she sits back down and she looks at me. *Kid, you gotta get out, move on, find your freedom now while you can. Those fuckers will leave you, they all do, believe me. Those fuckers are scared of women like you and me.* I smile and am about to ask her if she hears the voices also when she turns to yell at the barmaid, who is blocking her view of the TV screen. Hazel takes another smoke out of my packet, gets up and walks over to the young woman who was swaying to the music. I watch them talking together, see the young woman put another coin in the jukebox, hear Oasis come on and watch as they hold hands and jump up and down with joy.

I grab my bag and head to the toilet, one wobbly step after another. (I remember reading years ago that high heels were originally made for men during times of war. A man on horseback steadied in the stirrups when wearing them, his weapons used with balanced ease. Function, not fashion. The transformation of warfare in a rising and steadied foot.) I am one foot after the other, rising, falling and kicking open the toilet door. I am two feet steadied in front of the dirty, cracked mirror and looking at myself. A woman about to start a mighty war. My lips are a blazing pink, my arms are tumbling, are escaping out of the dress – fold over fold over fold. I move closer to the mirror and look for marks on my face, for mourning lines that I am certain will start to form soon. I place my bag on the bench and walk into the cubicle, hover over the toilet seat (a trick my mother taught me; a trick I guess your mother might have taught you too), piss warm-hot-too-yellow-dark-yellow-you-need-more-water-yellow into the bowl. I watch myself in the mirror as I wipe and stand up, pull my underwear up, pull down my dress, wipe the piss off that has trickled down to the back of my knees with my left hand. The largest crack in the mirror runs all the way down the middle of my body and I reapply my lipstick, pick up my bag and walk back out into the bar, to. My stool, to. Another schooner of beer waiting for me, to. The barmaid smiling with her hands on her hips and talking to a young man, to. The young man lifting his beer to his lips and turning to me, smiling. To, *Hey, Cyn, fancy seeing you here.* To, *Remember me? From work? Johnno? Jeez, you look a lot better than you did last time I saw you* (mud, birds' nests, feather, twigs – a night out on the land will do that to you, buddy). To, *Let's have a drink together.* To sitting right down next to me. To ordering us each a tequila shot. To another. To more beer. To me telling him things I'll never remember. To ordering hot chips with gravy – *soaking up all the booze, mate, soaking up all the booze.* More tequila. Another pack of smokes, a clean glass ashtray – ripping the foil off the top of the packet is one of my greatest pleasures, I think. I don't really listen to anything he says. I buy pork crackling in a metallic pink bag. I don't share it with him. (The comfort of weight on my bones – hold it all in), and. My hand on his leg, knees pressing up against his. *I like a young man*, I whisper in his ear, leaning over and slightly brushing up against his chest. In the corner, Hazel is now standing alone under a fluorescent light. The jukebox plays a slow Janis Joplin song. She is standing and staring at me as I turn to look at her. *Go. Go. Go*, she mouths to me from across the room. In his ear. I tell him that I want to fuck him. He tells me he has always wanted to fuck a curvy woman, a crazy woman and. His is the only voice that I can hear. He has no idea.

I take Johnno by the hand, lead him into the bathroom, push the bin up against the door so no one will come in (they won't, they all know what's happening in here). I don't say a word. I lift myself up onto the bench and pull my dress up, pull my underwear down. Mumble something about knowing what I want. I rub my hands up and down my inner thighs as he takes his dick out of his pants, moves in, pushes in, watches himself in the mirror as we fuck. (I hear the grunts of women, their pleas to stop, I hear the short breath of those coming, I hear *please* and *thank you*, I hear a father's footsteps coming to a daughter's bed, I hear a woman taking direction on a film set, her mouth set wide with metal bands.) He keeps moving in, out, harder, faster, my head banging on the mirror, the crack running down it now splintering across its width. I'm breathing heavy in his ear – *Tell me you like it, Johnno.* I push, push, I let my legs fall open as he pulls out and stands in front of me, does up his zip – *Fuck that was good, Cyn.*

I sit on the bench with my legs wide open, feeling him drip out of me (so much pleasure in holding and then letting go of his salted valour). *I've never fucked a ranga with red pubes before.* He waits for me to respond, and I stand up, lean over to the basin and turn on the tap, cup warm water in my hand, lean over and splash water up into me – wash him out of me, wash him out. The numb glory of it all. The art of war. He stands leaning up against the wall and watches, asks me if that's something women usually do. I ignore him. I walk into the toilet cubicle and wipe myself with toilet paper – scratchy, thinly, largely, small. Pick off the flinty bits that stick in my pubic hair. I put my underwear back on, pull down my dress, and I stand in front of the mirror fixing my hair. *Did you want to go out next week?* he asks, standing behind me. I ignore him and walk towards the door. *We could get a pizza or something.* I move the bin, stand there with my elbow ready to push the door open, and. I think of the ways in which love can start for men like Johnno, of the ways in which men want women they don't know, the ways women want men and men want men, and all the ways we want each other. I think of how men wanted my mother, of the idea of women loving women, how. My sex is my power, how my gender is a burden, so often attached to my anatomy. (*Girls are weak, chuck 'em in the creek; boys are strong, like King Kong* – my father laughing. *You feel just like your mother* – George's moussaka breath on the side of my face. *Mate, move to the side and show us her face, will you?* Faster. Faster. Back and forth. Forward, in the coldroom. Cameron. Salted salty salt.)

*You know, Cyn,* Johnno says as I push open the bathroom door, *Cameron at work says you're just as crazy as your mother, says he's seen you talking to yourself. Keeps threatening to teach you a lesson. I'd watch out if I were you. Have you seen the way he treats the bloody cattle in the stun box?* I tell him that he needs to stop listening to men like Cameron – that tough, that fearless women don't put up with shit that's said about them for very long. I feel blood rush through my body as I walk back out to the bar, feel the skin around my knuckles tighten as I make fists – anger rising with a whole history sitting under my skin. Johnno walks beside me and tries to take my hand. *Shit, Cyn, I probably shouldn't have told you that, should I?* I pull my hand away from his, and realise that he has no idea what Cameron and his mates did to me, what George did, has no idea of the power I possess.

THREE FLIGHTS UP. FOUR DOORS DOWN. NUMBER THIRTY-FOUR. The key slides in the lock, and. I'm inside and taking off my clothes. I'm standing beside the basin. I am taking a cup out of its thin paper sleeve and putting it under hot running water. I am lathering my hands with the soap and rubbing off Johnno's smell. My skin folds over itself, crowds my body (hold it all in). My hips are like the great dunes of the Simpson Desert, my arse the size of Uluru (no climbing this, fellas!). My hands are large and work-hard, my fingers open wide like the view from the front steps at home. My arms move up and down like slow-moving clouds heavy with rain as I soap my body. My eyes are wide in knowing. My neck is a bottle tree. Perhaps grief is a thing we can measure, I think: kilos on our bodies; metres and kilometres of the mapped world around us, the pressure of sound on surfaces, the temperature on your skin. I put my hands under the hot water and wonder if Uluru was picked up and weighed, what immense number would it be, and would we even have the collective heart to understand it?

THE NEXT MORNING, I check out of the hotel and put my bag in the ute. I light a smoke and walk up to the mall, get coffee, a meat pie from a bakery, make small talk with the young woman dressed in white behind the counter. She nods and smiles as I mention the weather (what I really want to say to her is: *Hey there, I'm starting a movement, a revolution, want to join me? Let me tell you about the women who've come before us*). She nods and smiles as I ask her name. *Next!* She starts serving the woman who was standing behind me as I leave.

At the newsagency a few doors up, I buy a newspaper with the report of a death of a young girl in Bundaberg on the front page – her body found slumped up against a tree near a dry creek bed. (Kathy is her name.) At the second-hand store a few doors down I buy a tortoiseshell hairbrush. (Charlotte used to own it, and she tells me that every night she would brush her hair a hundred times before bed for good luck, but that didn't help her on the night of the school formal.) I buy a pair of earrings that look exactly like the pair my mother used to have. (Her favourite pair – those silver flower studs.) I find an old purse on a wooden bench in the middle of the mall with nothing in it but a picture of a small child dressed in pink. (It was Katrina's.) At the Myer Centre, I look up past the escalators at the new cinema that has recently replaced the famous theme park on the top floor – the dragon roller coaster and the swinging pirate ship that I'd seen pictures of in the paper now gone. I take the lift up to the second level and walk into a store that sells make-up and perfume, buy a headband in a plastic wrapper. On the front of the packet is a smiling Korean girl. (It's Aera. She tells me her name means 'love'; that she lost her mother and father when she was just eleven; that for years she looked after her four brothers, who were at school; that her back ached from washing and cleaning all day.)

Outside, under the sun, I walk across a bridge over the Brisbane River – the same snaking brown river my mother watched on the day she met my father. As I enter the State Library (all sharp-edged concrete), I feel the coolness it contains, see my reflection as I look down at the large white tiles under my feet. There's a group of schoolkids sitting around a table reading comics. There's a homeless man without any shoes on pretending to read the paper while trying to sleep in a big leather chair, and. I walk up and down the rows of books and place my index finger on each one that was written by a woman. At the counter near the entrance, I ask the young woman if she knows how many of the books in their collection women wrote. She looks at me for a long time without answering. I stand firm, waiting, watching her lips move with a quiet mumble that I can't really hear or understand. (*Here's the red-headed woman from the bar last night, the one who fucked that young bloke in the toilets, who broke the mirror. My friends and I watched her all night. She even tried to talk to us. She might be really lonely but is probably just a slut.*) The woman starts typing into her computer, doesn't look at me. *You know,* she says to her fingers, *no one has ever asked me that before. I guess we just don't group the books in terms of gender. We do have a women's display on the back wall – mostly it's just cookbooks, though.*

THE HOT BREEZE HITS MY FACE – so much humidity, and my hair sticks to my face as I leave the library. I put the headband on.

It's green, Mallory's favourite colour, and. I walk back across the river, all the way back to the HQ. Too many steps to count, and. I'm. Pulling out of the vacant lot and driving. I'm driving past All Hallows', the Catholic girls' school that has been here since the 1800s. I'm stopping at a set of lights, look to the right at the grey metal body of the Story Bridge and hear the rhythmic sound of car tyres hitting the bridge's bitumen joins. Green light, turn left, keep driving. I still smell of Johnno. I open my legs wide and turn on the fan to try to dry him out of me (like a soldier sitting after a long day of battle, his legs spread and drinking a flask of cheap whisky). *Classy.*

# DON'T FUCK WITH WHAT YOU
# DON'T UNDERSTAND

I WAIT FOR THE FIRST BEAST to land on the bench, sharpening one knife at a time. Thuy, Maggie and Kim are on the other side of the platform, wearing their whites and looking over at me. *Ladies*, I yell over to them, *hope you're all well.* They stop staring and start to slice, giggle when a group of men walk past behind them for their smoke break. I pour oil on my sharpening stone, roll my knife over it again. (*An easy clean slice; one slice shows you know what the fuck you're doing*, my father used to say.) I slice a beast through the centre of its backbone, holding the knife in my fist. One slice down. I feel my heels lift from the floor. Push the ribs down with my large bulk. (That breaking bone sound.) I take a smaller knife and slice through the ribs. Left, right – a rhythm in my work. I'm still as fast as any man in here. I don't fuck around. There isn't a cut on any part of my body, and. My father, he'd be so proud.

I SEE CAMERON in the tearoom mid-morning. I'm drinking black tea from one of the only cups without a broken handle and eating a handful of Iced VoVos. He comes in all sweaty and sits beside me, sly-winks at two men walking in for the free biscuits. *Hey, Cyn.* I look down into my cup of tea, see it as a brewing tempest (an oncoming hurricane, a building tidal wave, a threatening earthquake, the moment before the Big Bang). I wish he would just fuck off. *So how's Johnno?* I look up at him. *Piss off, mate.* I get up and loom over him, so close that I can smell his oceanic smell. I am. Solid tallow. I am. Gristle. As tough as any man. As tough as him. Tougher. (Grief is a thing we can turn inside out, I think – use it as a weapon, as an almighty defiance, as the force behind the knife sliding down the torso of a beast.) He looks me straight in the eye, pulls back when he sees everyone watching us. *Fuck off,* he says to me, louder than he should in here. Maggie and Kim, without Thuy, walk in and go to the fridge, take out their small plastic containers full of rice and meat, stand together and put their containers in the microwave one at a time. They move to the far end of the long table and set out their containers to share, take chopsticks from a bag and start talking to each other with their mouths full. I look over at them and smile and then look at Cameron, who's leaving the room. *Cameron, mate . . .* He looks back at me, a certain wariness in his face (the first time I've seen it in him). *Don't fuck with what you don't understand.*

I hear on the radio that thunderstorms have hit in the east of the country, with winds so strong that they have ripped the roofs off houses. Spot fires have started popping up and a dust storm is heading our way. Pat enters the tearoom and leans down so his good ear is close to the radio, as Terry and Damo – two blokes who've only been here for a few months – walk in. *Hey, Cynthia, how's things?* A trepidation as they move around me to get to the fridge. I grunt and go over to the bench with the tea cannister and put another teabag in my cup, put it under the hot water. I watch as the steam rises, and I leave without saying a word, get back behind my bench and spend the rest of the afternoon cutting out bruises from the flanks of beasts and draining warm blood down the sink. Legs spread. Gloves on. A slice right through the belly of a beast.

IN THE AFTERNOON I WASH MY KNIFE, place it on top of the sharpening block and leave the cutting and boning room. It takes forty-seven steps to walk down the hallway to the back door for my break, and twenty steps until I see Cameron out of the corner of my eye through the dirty window, his hair standing up from the wild-warning-wind outside and his body leaning in, standing close, too close, to Thuy. She's alone with him out there, and he's pressing her up against the doorway of the toilet block. She's looking around – for Maggie and Kim . . . for anyone, I guess. She's trying to push him away, moving her head from side to side, and. I know what this is. I know how this begins, how this ends for her. (Australia has vast amounts of salt underground, built up over thousands of years. In some parts of the country the amount of salt is so immense that it will take once-fertile land generations to recover. Some land never will.)

I pick up my pace and push through the back door. *My name is Helen*, a woman says in my ear. *My sister Charlotte used to brush her hair with that brush you bought in the city.* I walk over to Cameron and Thuy. I'm heavy feet, I'm wide body, lowering my head and moving in like a fucking raging bull. I'm seeing him turn to me and pull away from Thuy, and. Cameron's walking towards me, his steps long, his chin high. My eyes heavy-close as I listen to the voice of another woman – *Oh, my head is so very sore, so very sore.* She's slow-drawling her words, and. I open my eyes when I smell Cameron's salty salt. *What else am I expected to do when those crazy whores cock-tease me all day, eh, Cyn? Maybe*

*I should take her out to that bushland you bloody love so much and give her a once-over like I did to you in the coldroom, eh?* Heat spreads through my chest, swells and expands as I press up against him. *Feel the fire, you fucker, feel the fucking firestorm*, I hear a woman scream, and. I'm not sure if it's me or one of them. I hold his wrist tight. Feel excitement building in me as I twist it. *Cyn!* It's Mallory, talking to me in the differing tones of ageing. *He's a bad man. He's coming for you. He's coming for us – twist it.* Oh Mallory, and. I move my groin up against his. Twist his wrist hard, harder. Hold him in a space he isn't comfortable with. Knows he's now being watched by Thuy and a group of men who've just walked out for a break, the men he often sits with at lunchtime, the ones I've heard him promise so many things to: throwing buckets of blood on me, making sure they all get a go of me in the coldroom. *Don't tell Johnno, though, fellas – the kid's too young for that kinda fun.* Cameron has explained that these are the consequences for women working in jobs that were made for men, I think, for existing in the places that were made for men, and. His eyes are wide (a man who is scared but won't admit it, a man your mother/your sister/your best friend/ the woman at a party once warned you about), as a big gust of wind races through and lifts up an overflowing rubbish bin, topples boxes full of old aprons sitting by the back door, whips a man's smoke from his hand. I hear a window slam shut and shatter inside the abattoir. And, the men watch us. And, Thuy starts coughing up the red dirt that's swirling all around us. The air is a dry-heavy weight, and. Cameron is a confused little boy standing in front of me, feeling the brewing furore in my body and the raged energy surrounding us. *I'm not fucking putting up with your bullshit anymore, mate*, I say, loud enough so everyone can hear me. Slide my nose up the nape of his neck and let out a ripe, rupturing groan. *You know not to fuck with me anymore.*

Thuy walks over to us and, ignoring Cameron, says, *Thanks, Cynthia. Thanks.* Together we walk away from him back to the abattoir, and she holds the door open for me. As we walk down the hallway, I am. A swaggering gait with an unlit smoke hanging out of my mouth and blood pulsing through my body. We walk into the cutting and boning room and stand behind our benches, facing each other. I am. Sharpening a knife and watching Thuy talking with Maggie and Kim. A half-beast falls in front of me. I lift my knife, see the three women looking over at me and smiling, mouthing, *Thank you, thank you.* In this moment, I am brave enough to talk with them about starting an uprising – *watch me.* I am. Walking over to their bench. I am. Asking them if they'd like to come with me on our next break to my special spot behind the old sheds. They all nod yes. They all say my name as I walk back to my bench, wave when I turn to look at them. I'm. Picking up a knife. I'm. One clean slice though the breastbone of the beast. I'm. Hearing a group of older women in my ear (*revolt, revolt, revolt*). And I know they are, an. Impatience, a. Wild reckoning, are. Excited about the others on their way, heading from the east, and all of us gathering momentum for their impending arrival.

# I REALLY WANT YOU TO KNOW

(HOW MANY TIMES have you heard a woman be called hysterical, crazy, impractical, a lunatic – her madness thought to be caused by the moon? How many times have you heard a man tell a woman to settle down, to chill, to not get her knickers in a knot, heard him ask if she is on her period? How many of these women are actually mad, do you think? How many of these women are just responding to being ignored or spoken for, are misplaced without hope of movement? No wonder they/we/you/I am. Angry. I want you to know, I really want you to know, that we are ready to start this.)

# TOGETHER, WE EAT MEN LIKE AIR

PAT STANDS WITH ME OUTSIDE THE ABATTOIR with his hands flat on his back, moving his hips backwards and forwards just like my father used to. *Looks like this dust storm is gonna hit us, Cyn*, he says to me, as I'm trying to light a knock-off smoke by putting my lighter under my shirt and sticking my head under my collar – smoke dangling from my mouth. I light it and look up to see Thuy, Maggie and Kim pull out of the car park in their station wagon, their long black hair untied and billowing out the windows. Pat stands up straight and starts rolling his own smoke. In my first week here I'd asked him where he thought my father might have ended up, and I remember that he had put his hand on my shoulder and said, *He probably just needs a break*

*after . . . well, after . . . after all this shit that's gone down, don't
you reckon?* I never asked him about my father again. We stand
together now in silence at the back door.

*Go on, Cyn, ask him – ask him now.* Mallory is still with me, is
a soft whisper in my ear. *So, what part of Brisbane does he live
in?* I ask, as Pat finishes his smoke and throws the butt on the
ground. *Who, love? Who would I bloody know in the city?* I feel
my chin rising at him like I'm ready for a fight. *My father, Pat.
I know you're still mates. I saw you. At the Criterion. In the beer
garden.* He rolls another smoke and lights it with his Zippo; offers
me the packet. *No, I'm good. So, what's his kid's name? And the
woman – who is she?* He takes a long drag of his smoke to give
him time to think about what to say. He blows the smoke out
slowly as he lowers his head and kicks a stone across the ground.
We stand there in that slow time I know so well out here. I don't
move. I don't say another word. I wait for him to respond. He
doesn't. I start walking to my ute, knowing he's not going to
tell me what I need to know. But as I get in the HQ, he starts
slowly walking over to me. When he reaches the ute he puts his
hands on the roof as I wind the window down. *Love, he just asked
me to keep an eye on you, to make sure you were okay. I don't get
involved in all that other stuff.* He pulls away and stands with his
hands by his sides. As I start up the ute, I see Cameron getting
in his car – an old, but well-maintained, black-and-white Torana.

Perfect body. Always clean and not a scratch on it; the kind of car that men stand around in groups and talk about. He puts his boots up on the dashboard and he's smoking. He's. Waiting. He's. Watching. Me. I slow down when I pass him, smirk at him, put my foot on the accelerator and drive, hear him try to start the Torana. It doesn't turn over. I hear him try again. Nothing. In my rear-view mirror I see him get out and open the bonnet, kick the front tyre. I hear him scream, *The battery's fucking dead.*

I AM. DRIVING OUT OF THE CAR PARK, and I suspect that the women will hit here very soon as a collection of outrage. I am. Driving out of town and looking in the rear-view mirror at the dust storm that's now fast approaching. Like a wall of fouled clouds, orange-red fairy floss moving over the land. I am. Hearing a mutiny of women's howls in the distance. A looping distress. A natural siren, as I move through a twilight-darkening-haze. Know that they are looking for Cameron, that he is probably still sitting in his car – such force, such fury for him. I drive like I am on the set of *Mad Max* (*I am the Nightrider. I'm a fuel-injected suicide machine. I am the rocker, I am the roller, I am the out-of-controller*) and the hot air rolls through my copper-gold-rusted hair, my flames rising out the window, rushing against the fading glow (like a cheetah running across plains, like a marlin after silver fish, like a greyhound in his first bloody race – the depth-charge howl). Dust rises as small dark cylinders in the headlights on the bitumen in front of me.

I PARK AT THE HOUSE AND RUN UP THE STAIRS, unlock the front door and quickly shut and lock it behind me. Find anything heavy: the couch, the table, chairs, my father's nightstand, a large bag of flour, plants; pile them up against the windows to stop them shattering from the force of the approaching winds. I gather hand towels, bath towels, sheets. Soak them under the tap in the kitchen sink. Wring them out, roll them up, place them at the base of the front door, the back door, on the windowsills (a trick I learnt from my father). The back room's tangled thicket has become an excited riot. They are dropping their leaves on the floorboards, they are breaking their pots, they are fast-growing and twisting together in enthusiasm for what they know has just happened to Cameron back at the abattoir. The ivy has crept over the floor and has started to climb up the walls – a new generation of living that I'll never know. *My baby girl,* I say out loud. Together, here, their murmur, their patter, their hum is all around me. *Don't worry, Cyn, the others aren't going to head this way. They just want to scare him,* a woman with a faint Liverpudlian accent says. She keeps talking to me like she knows me: *He cried out for his mother when all visibility was lost, curled up on the floor of his car whimpering.* I put down the armful of

240

cushions I'm holding and listen, trying to work out who she is. *You should have seen our dear Mallory, jumping up and down on the bonnet of his car – she's got some strength for a young one. Must be all that Scouser blood in the family.* There is the soft sound of water in her throat. *Grandma?* I say. *Is that you?* She doesn't hear me. *We made him understand though, dear, that he shouldn't mess with one of our own.* I hear water rushing and her gasping to get out her next sentence – *They've totalled his c—* And she is lost to the deluge.

I unlock the front door and walk out onto the verandah. The land around me is a velvety hush, a night-time cinema, a cin-e-matic parade full of swaggering soft shapes – a playground for them all. The women who were at the abattoir are now, I suspect, long gone from there and are making their way to where the land meets the ocean. I feel a soft breeze hit my face, feel the cool of another's palm in mine. It's Mallory, her small waxy hand still fitting so perfectly. She has come home to me. She is with me. She stands beside me and whispers, *Cyn, together, we eat men like air.*

# WE'VE GOT YOUR BACK

THE ABATTOIR'S buildings are covered in thick yellow-brown dust from the storm as I drive into the car park the next day. Someone has drawn a cock and balls on the side of the boss's van, and Cameron is standing beside his car, the bonnet crumpled like a chip packet. The back windows are smashed. The tyres are flat, and. As I grab my bag and get out of the HQ, I am welcomed by a cacophony, a rich aria, a great movement of women who are hollering at me from the bushland. A shattering of greens: emerald, sage, olive, mint, lime – all their radiant hues as broken light beaming out towards me. I hold my right hand up to my eyes to shade them from the glare as Cameron puts his hands on his hips. Steps into my path. Widens his feet. Stands his ground. I will take this fucker out if he doesn't move, I think to myself. (Chicken, chicken, who's gonna move out of the way first?) He moves just before I walk into him, and. He starts waving his arms, goes red in the face. He's all fists in the air and *you're a fucking slut*, as I pass him. I'm one finger up behind me as I keep walking. I'm. Copper-gold-rusted hair as explosion in the wind. I'm *fuck you, buddy*. I'm laughing and imagining Mallory beside me; we're holding hands, like Thelma and Louise did as they flew into the Grand Canyon. I'm about to walk in the back door, and. Mallory. She's here. She's a hoot, she's a razz, she is the belly-bellow laughter of a thousand happy women – *I love you, big sis*. I'm smiling up at the sky as I press my knee on the door to push it open. I'm open-mouthed amusement, a whole flock of sound rising. I'm your mother, your sister, your best friend. I'm the woman you met one night at a party who told you she was ready to change everything.

AT MORNING TEA TIME, before I go out for a smoke, I find the boss and ask him for a double shift, tell him that I need the cash, that rego on the ute is due, that I could do with a new set of knives. He moves his shoulders from side to side in ageing discomfort and says no, that the owners told him a few days ago that there was to be no more overtime and no new staff either. *Tough times,*

*Cynthia. This place is bloody falling apart.* He pats me on the back and walks out to the yard as a new batch of beasts are loaded in.

I follow him outside and head to the back sheds, notice that the dust storm hasn't touched the bushland; has skirted around it in loving restraint. Twenty more steps to the water tanks, and. I can hear a loud frenzy of women wild-screaming my mother's name in the distance, feel her head being slammed back and forth inside what I can only imagine is a metal toilet bowl in the hospital's bathrooms, hear water splashing around her submerging head, a deafening crack and a button pushed, her last gulping breath taken in a flushed-cyclone. I feel the beating heart, the pounding fists in my stomach of my little unborn Ivy – a loss, a never, a. Probably for the best. Mallory, I hear her also, and she tells me that she just wants to go home. Other women – Abigail, Britney, Eva, Jodie, Joanne – are shouting, *Watch out! Stop! He's coming, Cyn. There. There he is,* and.

THERE HE IS. There's Cameron walking slowly around the edge of the bushland flicking a red lighter. He's looking in. He's grabbing at the low-hanging wattle. He's wondering what all the fuss is about, I guess. Why I come here. What's in here that matters to me. Doesn't take long for someone to come and take something that isn't theirs, I think. Doesn't take long for women to rise together in anger, either. Doesn't take long to stop these kinds of men in their tracks. *Fuck him up, love, we've got your back* – I'm sure it's the voice of Hazel from the bar in Brisbane, and I wonder how she died, if it was of natural causes. In front of me, Cameron looks up, looks to his left, right, steps in. Trips over a small bush as the loose red dirt whirls around the edges of the bushland – like a smokescreen, a concealment, a place for things to go unnoticed. He is. Now moving in a place where he doesn't belong.

I lean against the wire fence that surrounds the water tanks and take off my boots, walk quietly up to the edge of the bush in my socks. Listen to another woman speaking to me: *She's always running around, that sister of yours. Always trying to catch fairies in jars. We don't have the heart to tell her that fairies don't exist. I saw her this morning. She's got the same hair colour as you – like fire. It's a dead giveaway of how she got here.* I stand with my hands on my hips and look for Cameron, hear him step on what I imagine is an old fallen tree, the crack as it breaks under his foot. I feel my muscles, my skin, tighten with rage. What the living fuck is this? I think. *Who the fuck does he think he is?* I say it aloud as I spot him standing in the place where I burnt golden leaves for Mallory. Listen – *Go on, Cyn, go get him.* I see a fog of bodies surrounding him. One woman is standing beside him like a guard, her face caved in by what looks like a hammer blow. One has blood running down the inside of her thighs as she crouches under a fallen branch throwing sticks at him. One limps behind a tree close to him and spits heavy phlegm on the ground. Cameron starts kicking the ash and dirt beneath him. Reaches up and pulls leaves from trees, staghorns from trunks, bends down and starts pulling up an autumn fern, bending its coppery fronds, and. He stops all of a sudden and stares at what he thinks is a ghost, an odd reflection of light, an illusion of the land. And Mallory. He sees Mallory. Her skin is stiff and shiny-white. Her lips are missing. Her skin is full of lines (like a dried, cracked river). She breaths in heavy gulps, her windpipe near collapse. She is taunting him. All around. Up a tree. He runs to it. She isn't there. On the edge of a small puddle of water. She isn't there. In the hollow of a tree. Her laughter is the most beautiful thing I have ever heard. Birds take flight to it. Flowers open to it. The autumn fern is standing tall, its copper fronds the conductor of her electric sound. Leaves fall. Branches fall. Holes form in the ground. He is a man scared, a man running. A man afraid of all of us.

# A GRAND ENCOUNTER.
# A TERRIFYING SCENE.

A WEEK BEFORE CHRISTMAS, and it's the hottest it's ever been in the cutting and boning shed. The owners have declared that it is too expensive to keep the air conditioner running, have told the boss to make us work faster. They have no idea how exhausted we get when the heat devours us.

ON THE FRIDAY MORNING we line up in the tearoom, dripping sweat, ready to punch in for the day. A young woman we've never seen before stands beside the clock and asks our names. She gives each of us an envelope that holds a slip of paper, and we open them and see the dates we have worked for the abattoir and the money we are owed in entitlements. None of us say a word, and we all walk outside together and light our smokes. Pat comes to stand beside me. *Looks like this is it then, kid. Bound to happen – the place has been going to shit for years.* He places his arm around my shoulders. *Fucking bullshit.* Thuy, Maggie and Kim walk past us, nod at me and jump in their car, all talking loudly; none of us understand a word they're saying. Pat looks over at them. *I've got a fucking family to feed, you know?* I nod at him, and listen as the rest of the men talk about having to pack up and move on, having to take their kids out of school, go back to trying to make a living on the forsaken land.

The young woman who handed us the envelopes comes outside, doesn't smoke. She tells us that the abattoir will close in two weeks, and that the owners have organised a Christmas party to thank us for our good work over the years. *We'll set up a marquee in the car park the Friday after next, at the end of your last shift. You're welcome to bring your families.* We are all silent, staring at her. *Now, let's all get back to work – you're still on the clock until then.* She turns on her silver high heels and walks back inside. We are all silent, and I finish my smoke and walk back inside, stand behind my bench and start breaking the legs of young beasts.

—

THE MEN'S WIVES DROP OFF LUNCHES FOR US EACH DAY. There are men in suits. There is a rumour that the land has been sold off to a mining magnate (hot-flushed with the idea of finding gold). There are men all around me complaining about the heat. There are nine days left, and a newspaper article on the fourth page of a national newspaper with an old photo of Simon and me, happy and surrounded by the boys. We are holding up a sign that reads *Timm Brothers' Meats*, and the article says that overseas investors are buying up big in the region. There is talk between us of this place once holding our family's futures, and *fuck you's* and *cunts* and *bastards*, and. *How will I pay the mortgage? How will we survive out here?* Seven days now. Six, and. Cameron stands out the back of the abattoir at lunchtime most days and watches Thuy, Maggie, Kim and me walk off to the back sheds, one of them carrying an extra plastic container of rice and meat just for me. There are two days left, and. Then.


A MARQUEE GOES UP. A van arrives with imported beer. Pizzas. A barbeque with gas bottles and a jumping castle for the kids. There is such grand celebration at our loss, as. The men stand around in the heat in their whites drinking beer, making plans. Four strangers in suits stand alone under the marquee and pretend to belong. Thuy, Maggie, Kim and I sit at a small wooden table. We've each got a paper plate with a large steak and some potato salad (barbeque sauce, lots of pepper – the meat a bitch to saw through with plastic knives and forks). We talk to no one but each other. Cameron sits near us on an old milk crate, and I hear him strike his lighter again and again. He's a confused and angry man, and. I look over at him as he crosses his arms and stares straight back at me, think that he doesn't know how fear works in his body, has probably never experienced it before. I get up and walk past him, closer than I should, to get some more potato salad. His smell (like a salt lake, a place where plants and animals cannot survive) is stronger than ever (a salt lake – an arid place that lacks an outlet to an ocean) and his sweat falls to the ground in front of him in large drops, his shirt soaked through.

LATE IN THE AFTERNOON, a handful of us decide to walk through the sheds for one last look. Cattle left half dead on the ground. Sharpening stones ripped off the tables – taken home for wives, I guess. Bloodstained aprons thrown on the floor. The coldroom door wide open, the space empty, as I walk in with Thuy, Maggie and Kim and pick up a meat hook left on the floor; hang it on the belt of my work pants like some kind of souvenir. Outside, Cameron wipes his face with his shirt. Strikes his lighter twice. A pool of sweat spreads between his feet, as. The men in suits leave, as. The marquees are packed up, and the other boys walk to their cars. This will be the last time they leave this place. *Fucking boss cunts. Let's go get on the beers, boys. Just in time for the topless meat tray draw – missus ain't gonna know what hit her when I get home tonight, eh?* As the four of us women walk out the abattoir's back doors, I hear Pat ask the others where Cameron is. No one knows. He's not sitting where he was, and. They're all standing at the open boots of their cars and changing into clean shirts, putting on their thongs, getting behind their steering wheels, and putting their cars into drive. They are pulling out of the car park, one after the other, a. Moving parade of the redundant and quickly forgotten.

*Maybe you'll all head up to the pub too, ladies,* the blokes who are still standing around say. I reach into my bag and pull out my smokes. *Yeah, maybe – just got a few things to do up near the sheds first.* To do: Explain to Thuy, Maggie and Kim what the bushland holds, introduce them to the other women there, teach them to sing Mallory's favourite lullaby, build new effigies, gather bright objects to attract her, and let her tell us all the places I once promised her we would visit together – the Left Bank in Paris, the ancient ruins in Rome, the pyramids in Egypt. Kiss her on the lips. Tell her: *Oh, Mallory, it's so good to see you,* and. Reach for, hold each other's hands, all of us – the living and the dead. Together, listening to each other. Finding comfort. Holding. Holding on. *Okay then* – the men nod at us and walk off to their cars, and. We're walking. We're one hundred and fourteen steps each before I begin to hear their surging and fertile vexed hum. Now closer, and their fists are beating at their chests in a constant loud rhythm. We are nearly there, and. There's a scream, a hiss, a shared bellow, a. *Ladies, look out he's here*, a. *He's got a lighter and a jerrycan of fuel*, a. Plea from Mallory – *Oh, Cyn, not again. Cyn, you have to stop it this time.* Thuy, Maggie and Kim come to a standstill when they hear them, look at each other and then at me. (They aren't afraid of anything.) *My sister*, I say to them. *Mallory*, and. They stand with me listening, to. Mallory, to. The voices of others, to. An urgent-toned woman who speaks in their mother tongue, and there is. A bright booming reckoning. Their smiles widening. An instant understanding of what this is. They nod, start giggling like excited schoolgirls, as Thuy points to the edge of the bush-land, where Cameron is sitting on a large chunk of granite. He doesn't see us. He's been there for a while now, I'm guessing. He's got a mustard-coloured jerrycan beside him, the red lighter in his left hand. We stand still, watching him, until my back starts to hurt (weight puts stress on the joints, makes the body hurt in ways I've never known), until Thuy grabs a large knife from her bag and holds it up in front of her. We start moving together, creeping towards him. We inch forward, our feet gliding over the hard ground. He has no idea what he's up against.

*Hey, mate. What's this then?* I say, as he turns to us, startled, jumps up when he sees the knife in Thuy's hand reflecting the dying sunlight, knocks over the jerrycan, and. Five steps. Ten. Run. He's running, and. We are slow-swagger behind him. We are women confident, unrushed and sure of ourselves. We are walking into the bush following the petrol smell that's on his boots, lifting our noses for the scent. *Hold tight, Cameron,* I yell. *We're coming for you* (we are the kind of women your father warned you about – watch us). We're. Finding him hiding behind a huge bunya tree. *What the fuck is with you, mate?* I say as he steps out from behind it, and. He's. Shaking like a leaf. He's. A shell of a man. He's. Quaking in his boots. His blood is. Running cold. He's. Ready to jump out of his own skin. His eyes are on Thuy's knife as I take the meat hook off my belt and stand on my tiptoes, hang it on a thick branch of the bunya above me. *Do you wanna know what it feels like for a group of women to break open your ribcage with their hands?* The canopy above us starts to shake, sheds its leaves on all of us. Cameron's pleading voice is a pair of broken drumsticks on cymbals, is an out-of-tune electric guitar, is a saxophone played by an amateur, as. The once hidden, the once beaten and ignored, begin to push up against his chest and lift him off the ground. His nose starts to run. Piss trickles down his legs. He looks around, has no idea what's happening, thrashes his body in defiance. Thuy, Kim, Maggie and I stand back, watching. I reach into my pocket and pull out smokes for each of us, light them and hand them around. Together, the four of us inhale and exhale deeply, groan deep sounds of luxury from our throats.

# THE WOMAN YOU COULD BE

IN THE ABATTOIR'S CHANGE ROOMS I turn the shower on and take off my boots and my work clothes, throw them on the ground. I stand under the nozzle and scrub my skin, lean my head back and open my mouth, swallow big mouthfuls of water. I hear Thuy, Maggie and Kim beeping the horn of their station wagon as they drive out of the car park, and I turn off the water and step out, use an old hand towel to dry myself, wring my hair over the sink. I dress in a pair of jeans and an old polo shirt that's been left on the clothes hooks on the wall, and. I'm. Two hundred barefooted steps to my ute. I'm. Leaving the car park and not looking back.

—

AS I DRIVE THROUGH TOWN, I see the young girls who were sitting on their bikes outside the church on the day of George's funeral. They're in front of the corner store now, drinking Cokes and holding on to the store's front wooden posts to keep their wheels steady. I feel the heat of the ute's seat burn the backs of my legs through my jeans, blood caked under my nails; see one of the girls lift her index finger slightly from the handlebar of her bike as I pass. I pick up speed. I am seventy, I am a hundred, I am a hundred and twenty kilometres an hour as I reach the wide-open road. I am all the grand possibility. I am. The woman you could be. I am. The woman they just might become.

# EPILOGUE

YOUR CALL TO arms, your readying, your blazing green light*: There is a list. You have a list too, don't you? Your/my mother does. Your best friend does. The woman you met at a party, the woman you've never met does. Yours is kept in your head, but while drunk one night you wrote all their names on a piece of foolscap paper; stopped when you got too drunk to care anymore. You never finished that list, are still not sure if you can remember all their names or descriptors. I am/you are/ they are misplaced. Your/my mother is. Your best friend is. The woman you have never met is. You've recognised yourself in these

_____

* *yes, yours.*

pages, haven't you? You've seen something that you remember. Different landscapes. Sounds. Smells. Different years. But the same in so many ways – wherever you are, wherever that is, wherever it could be. You have felt the earth change and move under your feet with our collective reckoning. It's unsettled you. It's moved you away/closer/indoors. It's made you feel unsure of it all (I want you to know, I really want you to know that you are not alone in feeling this). Men, if you don't recognise yourself in this tale, read it again. Find yourself in here. Read it from the start. Again. No. One more time. Take each page, each line, slowly. Roll words around in your mouth. Tell me you're a good man after multiple reads (the problem is that you all tell us that you're one of the good ones). Men. Get a pen. An old map. You will most probably find one in an unused drawer or folded inside an old book. You may even have to go to the store and buy one – the automobile club in your state, a tourist kiosk in the centre of your town, a real estate agent thinking you're in the market to buy, will all probably give you one for free. Get sticky tape. Walk into your bathroom and stick it to the wall beside your mirror. Write the names of every woman you have ever known on the map. Write where you met them. Write this in the colour of your choosing. Think of what they will most remember you by. Think on that. Stand and think on that. No, think some more. Now. Be honest. After you have done that for a full five minutes (no – make it ten), try to remember their stories. Did you listen to their stories? Or did you silence them? Did you care enough to ask? Listen for their voices. Start to say their names out loud. Watch yourself in the bathroom mirror doing this. Open your mouth wide. Hear the echo of your own voice in their names, in their tales up against the tiles and glass around you. Look yourself in the eye when you have done this. (It may take you hours, weeks, it may take you more than a year to do this. There may have been many women.) Open your mouth wider. Say to the mirror, to your reflection, that you will start to share our stories. (You can start with this one; it's the story of our collective grieving.) Share our stories with other men you know; with your brother, your father, with the men at the pub, with the man you met one night at a party. For God's sake, tell your sons. Tell them. Make them all promise to keep sharing them. (Think of this as a pyramid scheme, an Amway sale, a way for you to help us to build our power. Call it a goddamn tribute if you need to.) Sometimes these stories we tell won't be about you or the other men you know (be the good guy, show us that you are – go on); they'll be the stories we've inherited from our friends, our mothers, their mothers and all the mothers before them. Our bodies remember – the beatings, the losses, the knives at our throats, the hands on our breasts, the silence, the control, the beat, the hum, the slow-mouthed violence in our ears. They remember – the disdain, the back seats, the long ways home. You have built great empires, large institutions, clubs and codes to keep us out. Know this. Keep knowing this. Keep listening, and. Help us place ourselves in different ways. (Think of all the men who have discovered land, who reclaimed, burnt, gunned down, bombed nations. Think of the ways in which men police the lands we live on. It has been forever now, hasn't it? It's been going on for longer than it should have, right?) Help us to move in new ways, to build new meaning together, to run across the earth to each other. Let your bathroom be the place where this begins. One name at a time. That's it. Mouth the first name now. It's so very easy. Start the with beginning of the alphabet. *Abby, Amy, Andrea.* Listen for us as we amble, stride, run towards you. Hold your arms open when we arrive. Hear that? Yes? That's the sound of women huddled together making plans in lifeboats. Hear that? That's us high-tide rising around you. Hear this – this is the sound of revolution. We are coming, and we are ready.

# CREDITS

The quote 'Whenever you trying to pray, and man plop himself on the other end of it, tell him to git lost, say Shug. Conjure up the flowers, wind, water, a big rock' (on page 98) is taken from Alice Walker's *The Colour Purple*.

The lines 'my nose, my eye pits, my full set of teeth, smell my sour breath' (on page 96) and 'Together, we eat men like air' (on pages 237 and 241) are adapted from Sylvia Plath's poem 'Lady Lazarus'.

# ACKNOWLEDGEMENTS

*THE FURIES* was completed as part of a doctoral thesis in creative writing at RMIT and supported by an RTP Stipend Scholarship, as well as a Creative Victoria Sustaining Creative Workers Initiative Grant. Time spent in the beautiful isolation on the Williams River in New South Wales at Judith Emanuel's property also helped in the early development stages of the book. Other notable thanks go to the indomitable Dr Julienne van Loon (I am a better writer and critical thinker because of you. I will forever be grateful for your guidance, patience and your thinking beyond what is, to what could be) and Vanessa Radnidge (in what was the very worst of years, you were a voice of constant reason and kindness. The belief you have in the words I put on the page and my voice will always stay with me). Thank you also to my wonderful, picky, patient editors, Ali Lavau and Sophie Mayfield. This book is better because of you both. To my love, my Russ (you see my writing as real work, as valuable and important. Fuck, you're great. This short life we have together will never be enough for us.) To Richard, Di and Ben. I love you. Losing Angus last year was the hardest thing, but somehow we held each other together. I love you all. And of course, my darling boy Shankly, who was my constant writing companion, my best snuggle buddy and owned my whole heart. You really were the best boy, and we miss you every single day.

*The Furies* was written on the traditional land of the Wurundjeri people. Always was. Always will be.

Mandy Beaumont is an award-winning writer, researcher and book reviewer. Mandy's collection of short stories, *Wild, Fearless Chests*, published in 2020, was shortlisted for the Richell Prize and the Dorothy Hewett Award, and a story from the collection won the MOTH International Short Story Prize. She teaches at Griffith University in Creative Writing and is also a researcher at RMIT where she is engaging, through fiction, with the work of Simone de Beauvoir. For more information, visit www.mandybeaumont.com

 @mandybeaumont